I charge the borrowed magic sword, cloaking it in flame.

Then I swing the sword to deflect the Fireball.

The flames of the spell and the sword clash, igniting a massive explosion.

It burns! I can't breathe!

But I have to keep moving forward!

Just one more step!

Jeskan
[J]o adventurer who
[i] A rank on his own.
[A]ll kinds of weapons.

Julius
A hero chosen by the gods.
Possesses a beautiful
and noble spirit.

Hyrince
A member of Julius's party
and his close partner.
Often teases Yaana.

Hawkin
Once a famous gentleman
burglar known as the Thief
with a Thousand Knives.
Now Jeskan's slave.

Yaana
A saint. While serious
and honest to a fault,
she often makes
absentminded mistakes.

A s...
reache...
Uses ...

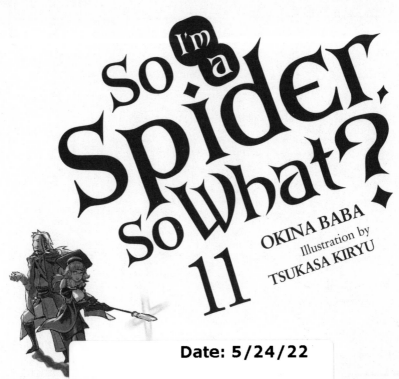

So I'm a Spider, So What?

11

OKINA BABA

Illustration by
TSUKASA KIRYU

YEN
ON
New York

So I'm a Spider, So What?, Vol. 11

Okina Baba

Translation by Jenny McKeon
Cover art by Tsukasa Kiryu

KUMO DESUGA, NANIKA? Vol. 11
©Okina Baba, Tsukasa Kiryu 2019
First published in Japan in 2019 by KADOKAWA CORPORATION, Tokyo.
English translation rights arranged with KADOKAWA CORPORATION, Tokyo, through
TUTTLE-MORI AGENCY, INC., Tokyo.

English translation © 2021 by Yen Press, LLC

Yen On
150 West 30th Street, 19th Floor
New York, NY 10001

Visit us at yenpress.com
facebook.com/yenpress
twitter.com/yenpress
yenpress.tumblr.com
instagram.com/yenpress

First Yen On Edition: March 2021

Yen On is an imprint of Yen Press, LLC.
The Yen On name and logo are trademarks of Yen Press, LLC.

Library of Congress Cataloging-in-Publication Data
Names: Baba, Okina, author. | Kiryu, Tsukasa, illustrator. | McKeon, Jenny, translator.
Title: So I'm a spider, so what? / Okina Baba ; illustration by Tsukasa Kiryu ;
    translation by Jenny McKeon.
Other titles: Kumo desuga nanika. English | So I am a spider, so what?
Description: First Yen On edition. | New York, NY : Yen On, 2017–
Identifiers: LCCN 2017034911 | ISBN 9780316412896 (v. 1 : pbk.) |
    ISBN 9780316442886 (v. 2 : pbk.) | ISBN 9780316442909 (v. 3 : pbk.) |
    ISBN 9780316442916 (v. 4 : pbk.) | ISBN 9781975301941 (v. 5 : pbk.) |
    ISBN 9781975301965 (v. 6 : pbk.) | ISBN 9781975301989 (v. 7 : pbk.) |
    ISBN 9781975398996 (v. 8 : pbk.) | ISBN 9781975310349 (v. 9 : pbk.) |
    ISBN 9781975310363 (v. 10 : pbk.) | ISBN 9781975310387 (v. 11 : pbk.)
Subjects: CYAC: Magic—Fiction. | Spiders—Fiction. | Monsters—Fiction. |
    Prisons—Fiction. | Escapes—Fiction. | Fantasy.
Classification: LCC PZ7.1.O44 So 2017 | DDC [Fic]—dc23
LC record available at https://lccn.loc.gov/2017034911

ISBNs: 978-1-9753-1038-7 (paperback)
        978-1-9753-1039-4 (ebook)

10 9 8 7 6 5 4 3 2

LSC-C

Printed in the United States of America

contents

J1   JULIUS, AGE 11: BEGINNINGS

When I was young, I loved the epic tales of heroes that my mother would read to me.

Hearing my beloved mother's gentle voice describe the great deeds of the heroes always made my heart dance.

Some were even based on heroes who really existed in the past, and I wanted to be just like them.

Banishing evil and protecting the weak…

I wanted more than anything to become a noble hero.

When I told my mother this, she simply responded with a smile.

"Of course. I'm sure you will, Julius."

I was so thrilled by her answer that I decided right then and there to devote myself to living up to the strong yet kind heroes of legend.

To always hold justice close to my heart and never allow evil to go unpunished.

Young as I was, I knew I had no real chance of ever becoming a hero, but I wanted to at least have the attitude of one so that I could be a good prince.

I never imagined that not long after that moment, I really would be a hero.

When it happened, I was more confused and nervous than excited, but my mother gently encouraged me.

"You only need to be yourself, Julius. After all, you're already my hero! Just having you close by gives me courage."

At the time, I was too flustered to tell her how happy those words made me.

And I would never get another chance.

Mother...to me, *you* were the real hero.

Even now, thinking of you fills me with the strength to go on.

I'm trying to be myself, to embody the kind of hero I believe in, like you always told me to.

But lately, I've been having doubts.

What if there are some obstacles in this world that no amount of ideals can surmount?

What should I do if I run into an impassable wall?

Mother, please give me just a little more of your courage.

"Expose a human-trafficking organization?"

"Yes, that's right. I would like you to spearhead the efforts as the hero."

The elderly man smiling gently before me is the leader of the Word of God religion, Pontiff Dustin LXI.

He looks like a perfectly normal old man, but there's an aura of holiness about him that makes his powerful standing incredibly apparent.

And yet, his soft smile is strangely reassuring. He isn't intimidating at all.

But while this pontiff seems like the ideal holy man, I don't like dealing with him.

I know he's not the kind and saintly man he appears to be.

My first battle—the war between Ohts and Sariella—has become a bitter memory.

Following the pontiff's orders, I participated in the fighting on the Ohts side.

Since victory was supposed to be certain and the dangers minimal, he suggested that I could at least experience what it felt like to stand on a real battlefield, and I accepted his invitation.

The hero has always acted with the support of the Word of God.

As such, there is a bond between the two that can never fully be broken, and requests from the Word of God are difficult to turn down.

Besides, at the time, I had no particular concerns about the offer, so I accepted without thinking about it too deeply.

The result of my blindness was the disaster that befell a town in Keren.

As the Ohts soldiers ravaged the place, the townspeople turned glares of hatred on me. Their warmhearted smiles were nowhere to be seen.

I endured not only their stares but every stone, kick, and punch they threw as well.

As the hero, I should be the representative of all humanity, but since I participated in a war between humans and chose a side, the natural implication was that the opposing side—the country of Sariella—must be in the wrong.

Only after I witnessed the destruction of the devastated town did I realize for the first time that I had misjudged my role as the hero.

My individual strength matters little in the grand scheme of things, but the title of Hero carries the weight of all the generations that came before me.

What people value is the concept of the hero, not me specifically.

In other words, whoever currently inhabits the role of the hero must carry the weight of every hero who has come before.

I'd allowed myself to be used because I failed to understand that properly.

Manipulated by Pontiff Dustin, the man standing before me.

"Are you aware that children all over the world have been disappearing without a trace? Our investigation has revealed that the culprits are part of a massive human-trafficking organization, one which transcends the borders between nations. In order to combat this criminal enterprise, the Word of God has created a special task force. And I would like you to lead that force."

The pontiff quietly continues his explanation.

I have been hearing quite a bit about young children being kidnapped in countless areas.

If it's the work of a human-trafficking organization, I definitely can't let that slide.

Kidnapping is a crime, and all the more unforgiveable if the children are being sold.

If what the pontiff says is true, that is.

"Do you have any documents about this organization? I'd like to take a look at them before I decide, please."

I won't give my answer right away.

I agreed to join the battle between Ohts and Sariella without thinking things through, and I've regretted it ever since.

Every action I take needs to be carefully thought out.

Instead of blindly doing whatever I'm told, I have to think about what a real hero would do.

This is also important to prevent others from taking advantage of my title again.

"But of course. I shall have them brought to you at once. I should also mention that the commanding officer of the force has requested to meet you. If you have the time, would you be willing to speak with them?"

"All right."

I part ways with the pontiff and go back to my room.

"Whew..."

As soon as I'm alone, I heave a sigh.

The Holy Kingdom of Alleius is home to the headquarters of the Word of God religion and has teleport gates linking it to every country of note.

Naturally, it also has a dedicated room that has been used by generations of heroes, located here for maximum coverage and access in case any emergencies arise.

These teleport gates are one of the reasons I can't ignore the Word of God if I am to continue acting as humanity's hero.

A few steps can bring me to a distant country on the other side of the continent in the blink of an eye.

I can go right from being on standby to helping the people who are in trouble moments later.

So no matter how wary I am of the pontiff, I cannot simply refuse to deal with him.

I think back on the pontiff's gentle smile.

Hiding behind that smile is a cold, calculating politician.

You would never know it by just looking at him, but the pontiff is willing to commit any atrocity if he deems it necessary.

That became painfully clear to me during the battle between Ohts and Sariella.

But that doesn't mean he's a force of absolute evil, either.

The pontiff never acts out of self-interest. Everything he does is for the sake of the Word of God faith and for the people who believe in it.

He takes actions befitting a man who rules over others.

Sometimes he even seems like what all kings should aspire to be.

He'll use any means necessary to accomplish his goals.

And his goals are never malicious or corrupt.

So while I'm bitter that he used me, I can't wholeheartedly hate the pontiff.

I know far too well from watching my father what duties come with being king.

There often comes a time when you have no choice but to make painful decisions for the sake of your people.

I am no fan of the pontiff, and I prefer to avoid him if possible, but I don't loathe him enough to refuse him outright.

That's my honest opinion of the pontiff.

Which is exactly why it's unsettling.

I was taken advantage of and witnessed the tragedy of Sariella firsthand, but the pontiff clearly doesn't fit the description of evil.

He acts in accordance with what he believes is right and does his best to see that justice is served.

If that is true, then what is justice really?

I don't understand.

What is the right thing for me to do?

A knock on the door pulls me out of my swirling thoughts, back into the present.

"Come in."

It must be someone bringing the documents about the human-trafficking group that I requested from the pontiff.

But when I respond, an unexpected person opens the door.

"Pardon me. It's good to see you again, Sir Hero."

A graceful middle-aged man bows smartly and enters the room.

His polished manners and fine clothes mark him as a high-ranking noble.

However, the well-defined muscles that are visible even through his shirt show that he's a seasoned fighter as well.

"Mr. Tiva! It's good to see you, too."

Tiva is a noble and soldier of the empire. He looked after me in Sariella.

"I am glad to see you in good health. My blood certainly ran cold when I heard of Lord Ronandt's latest exploits."

I force out a weak laugh at Mr. Tiva's playful joke.

I really did think I was going to die…

Even now, my master sometimes appears in my nightmares, cackling with his body wreathed in flames.

Enough. Just thinking about it makes me shudder.

"So what are you doing here, Mr. Tiva?"

I change the subject with a question I'm genuinely curious about.

Mr. Tiva is an important figure in the empire, so I doubt he would come all this way for no reason.

"Oh, you haven't heard? I am in fact the commanding officer of the special task force created to combat the human-trafficking organization. If you end up leading us, I shall serve as your deputy. Otherwise, I shall assume the role myself."

This is completely unexpected, at least to me.

"Mr. Tiva, you're acting as a commander for the Word of God?"

Tiva is a soldier of the empire. While the Word of God is the chief religion there, it seems rather unusual for a person from another nation to be heading up this force.

"Ah, yes. Your doubts are perfectly understandable. Various circumstances led to this curious development. Please allow me to explain."

With that, he gestures for me to sit.

I comply and settle on the sofa in the reception area, and Mr. Tiva takes a seat across from me.

"First, please have a look at this."

Tiva holds out a sheaf of papers covered in writing.

The topmost document contains the names of several nations, along with a certain set of numbers.

"These are the estimates of how many have likely been kidnapped by the human-trafficking organization."

"What?!"

I can't help but exclaim out loud.

This is far higher than anything I expected.

Even the lowest estimates are at least two digits, and they go up to three digits on the higher end.

The empire's number is so high that it almost requires a fourth digit.

"I'm afraid it's true. There has always been some degree of illegal human trafficking in the past. However, the amount of activity in recent years is beyond unusual. With more disappearances occurring throughout the world than ever before, we concluded that there must be an organization of unprecedented scope behind these kidnappings—a gigantic group determined to spread its evil influence across the world. And so the various realms have agreed to collectively combat the problem. If this league of villains has tendrils committing sinister deeds all over the world, then every nation has an obligation to work together to stop them. However, there are certain complications that come with an operation of this scope. Because of its influence over many different nations and it being the home of the main branch of the Word of God, the Holy Kingdom of Alleius was selected to take the lead on this whole endeavor."

Judging by Mr. Tiva's explanation, this human-trafficking organization is far larger and more dangerous than I had even imagined.

So much so that the only way to stop it was a special task force combining the powers of several states.

"No nation will openly complain about the Holy Kingdom of Alleius being in charge, no matter how they might feel privately. And you, being both the prince of the powerful Analeit Kingdom as well as the hero of humanity, are to be the commander. With myself, a soldier of the equally influential Renxandt Empire, as your right-hand man, we should be able to maintain a careful balance."

The Holy Kingdom of Alleius, the Analeit Kingdom, and the Renxandt Empire.

This combination of the three greatest powers would naturally silence virtually all complaints.

It's a very logical plan, typical of the pontiff.

And at the same time, I realize that I have no choice but to agree.

Considering how far things have already come, everyone involved must have already been informed that I'm the top candidate to lead the task force.

If I was to decline and Mr. Tiva became the supreme commander instead, I'm sure rumors would spread quickly.

It would be one thing if it was only my own reputation at stake, but that could cause trouble for my home country of Analeit as well.

I'm sure the people of other nations would jump to some damning conclusions about why I declined, including those critical of the kingdom itself.

That's the last thing I want.

Again, I am reminded that my life and decisions are not truly my own.

I have two roles: as the hero and as the prince of the Analeit Kingdom.

And I must never act in a way that would tarnish either title.

Any mistakes I make will not end with only my suffering.

I'd be dragging the names of past heroes through the mud and bring shame to the Analeit Kingdom to boot.

The weight of my title and prince-hood is not so trivial as to forgive my mistakes simply because I'm still a child.

The pontiff is perfectly aware of that and crafted a scenario that leaves me no room to refuse.

I can't say I'm surprised in the slightest.

"It doesn't seem as if I can decline."

As I heave a sigh and respond, Tiva smiles dryly at me.

"It appears you've stayed true to your resolve, seeing, thinking, and making decisions for yourself. That's an admirable thing."

"...Not that it matters, since my hand's been forced regardless."

Whatever my intentions are, the pontiff likely still sees me as a child who can be easily manipulated.

This series of events has only proven that to be true once again, which is deeply depressing.

But Tiva has a thing or two to say about my grumbling.

"Not that it matters? I would say it matters quite a bit. You are acting based on what you believe is right. That will not go unnoticed. I'm sure there will be many who decide to follow you because of your character. Such as myself, for instance."

Mr. Tiva winks at me.

I'm impressed that the playful gesture suits him so well, even at his age.

"You are the hero, but you are also an individual human being. There are those who see you for who you are and what you do, not just your title. And if you continue to think and act based on your personal sense of justice, people will naturally come to follow in your footsteps. I'm sure in time, that will prove to be a great source of strength."

I feel my perspective grow as I think on Mr. Tiva's words.

I'm a hero but also an individual.

That idea is the complete opposite of how I've been approaching my life all this time.

But Mr. Tiva is saying that my personal decisions are what's important, not my title as the Hero.

That I should gain more followers with my actions, not my status.

"And if those people prove to be truly trustworthy, so much the better."

Mr. Tiva smiles, but his words also seem like a warning that I shouldn't be too quick to accept people I'm not sure I can trust.

"At any rate, you have to build these things over time. Let more people see you in action and share your beliefs. No one will listen to someone without a proven record, no matter how loudly they shout. I'm sure there are people who would follow you based on title alone, but that isn't reliable. You need people who will stand with you because it's *you*. Now, you're still young and inexperienced, with few accomplishments to speak of. But that also means you'll have plenty of opportunities ahead of you. There's no need to rush. Just keep moving forward one step at a time."

Slowly...

It's true that I don't have nearly enough experience yet.

"Fortunately, there's no hidden dark side to this request. It's a mission of justice, to save people who are suffering because of this human-trafficking organization. You may not have enough of a voice to protest assignments from the Word of God just yet, but if you carry out these requests and amass successes, your fame is sure to rise. This request involves many different nations, too, so it's the perfect opportunity. Use it to your advantage instead of simply letting others use you. That, too, is a kind of strength that you will need."

This has been very educational.

Mr. Tiva's advice is just what I needed.

I should exploit the pontiff's requests as a stepping-stone, the same way he's been exploiting me.

"Still, you must be careful not to be fooled by sneaky adults. For example, you should consider how I might only be saying all of this because I want you to join the force."

Startled, I look at Tiva only to find him grinning teasingly.

From his expression, I can tell that he's half joking.

The other half is a warning.

As if to emphasize this, Mr. Tiva's smile fades into a serious expression as he continues.

"It's very important to lend an ear to the viewpoints of others. But you mustn't simply take everything they say at face value. You will have to think about it yourself and come to your own conclusions. What is right? What is wrong? Only after agonizing over these things will your answer have any worth."

In other words, never stop thinking?

"Now then, that's enough preachy lecturing from this old man."

"No, it was incredibly helpful. Thank you."

Mr. Tiva smiles kindly and hands me the other documents pertaining to the request.

"I'll let you have a look at these. Read them over, think long and hard, then decide for yourself whether to accept."

"I will."

Giving a satisfied nod at my response, Mr. Tiva at last leaves the room.

Decide for myself…

I'll review the documents and then make up my mind, like he suggested.

That said, in my heart, I've already decided what to do.

I'm going along for this mission.

If Mr. Tiva will be with me as my deputy, then there's nothing to fear.

I'll think, act, and press forward one step at a time.

So that I can live up to my vision of the ideal hero.

As I harden my resolve, I tightly clutch the scarf wrapped around my neck.

TIVA VICOW

One of the few and powerful survivors who fought in the war against the demons alongside Ronandt and the previous sword-king. As a result, he possesses prodigious influence over his troops, who have absolute faith in his strength. The current sword-king also trusts him deeply as his right-hand man. It would be no exaggeration to say that it is his support that buoys the sword-king. He is blessed with both brains and brawn. When commanding an army, his style is to overwhelm his opponent with his rock-steady strategies; when in combat, he can easily take on a thousand men by himself. The Renxandt Empire would be lost without him. However, because his son, daughter-in-law, and grandchild were killed by the human-trafficking organization, he has chosen to leave his homeland and seek revenge as part of the task force.

Sophia's Diary 1

I'm sooo bored.

I don't get to see Merazophis today, as usual.

White hasn't come back to the duke's mansion in a while, either.

She's off doing something or other with Miss Ariel, apparently.

It's not fair!

I'm bored to tears here. So bored, I could die!

The last time White returned from her little adventures, I complained about it to her, and the next day, she gave me a written training regimen.

Ugh! That couldn't be further from what I wanted!

I mean, yes, technically this gives me something to do, but still!

Besides, who would *want* to do something this insanely hard-core anyway?!

Isn't there another option?!

Like paying more attention to me!

J2 JULIUS, AGE 12: FIRST EXPEDITION

It's been about six months since I agreed to join the special task force for combating the human-trafficking organization.

That means the New Year has come and gone, and I'm a year older.

In those six months, the task force has been fully assembled, and we're finally setting forth to smoke out the organization.

The reason it took half a year to mobilize is because so many different nations are supplying soldiers for this mission.

Each nation has their own goals in mind, so it took quite some time to select who they would be sending, or so I'm told.

To be fair, it must be difficult to take swift action when there are so many varying interests and expectations to account for.

I understand that's unavoidable to a degree, but I can't deny that I've begun to feel restless.

Now that the long-awaited day has finally come, all I am is eager.

This is where it begins.

"Hey, Juliuuus! Tea's ready."

"How can you still speak to him so impolitely?! Childhood friends or not, to address Sir Hero by name so casually is quite unacceptable!"

As I sit in the lounge mentally preparing myself, I hear two people arguing. Their voices give it away that they're about my age.

Turning around, I see a familiar girl and boy approaching.

"Yeah, yeah. I'll be careful from now on or whatever."

"Honestly! What sort of attitude is that?! You don't intend to be careful in the least, do you?!"

The boy shrugs as the girl rages at him.

This sort of exchange has become a regular ritual lately.

The boy's name is Hyrince. He's from the Analeit Kingdom like me, and despite his lax attitude, he hails from the noble family of Duke Quarto.

However, since he already has an adult elder brother who's well-placed to take over as the next head of the family, Hyrince is in a bit of an odd position as the second son.

Among the nobility, a second son is often treated as a backup in case something should happen to the first, but in Hyrince's case, his elder brother already has a child of his own, so he's completely extraneous.

I can't help but sympathize, as I occupy an equally strange place in my family as the second son of royalty but born to a concubine.

That's probably why we've been close since we were very young.

So yes, you could call him my childhood friend.

He's one of my few close companions whom I've known since before I became the hero.

And now, Hyrince is coming along as my attendant. In essence, his job is to look after my needs.

It's not the kind of job that would normally be given to the son of a duke, second or otherwise, but since I'm royalty and the hero, I'm allowed exceptions like this.

In fact, if Hyrince hadn't come forward for the role, I probably would've been inundated with petitions from all over the kingdom and even other countries as people vied to get closer to me.

It was Hyrince's status as a person of importance from my homeland that allowed him to push aside the other contenders for this role.

I much prefer having a familiar friend by my side over someone I've never met, especially strangers who likely have political motives.

But there's one person who isn't so fond of his frank nature.

Namely, the girl who's been chewing him out since they entered the room: Yaana the saint.

The saint is a role that pairs with the hero.

However, instead of being chosen through a title like the Hero, they have to

undergo difficult training from a young age and meet certain qualifications to be selected.

In a way, candidates for sainthood must traverse an even more grueling path than heroes, so the person finally chosen for the role is an elite beyond any doubt.

At least, that's how it's supposed to be…

"Hey, Julius. Drink it before it gets cold, will ya? You gotta rest up while you can, or it's gonna be rough later."

"Hey! Don't you ignore me!"

…Hyrince's attitude toward her doesn't exactly make her seem that way, though.

The saint is usually dispatched by the Word of God religion to support the hero.

To say the saint is a mediator between the hero and the Word of God would be putting it kindly. In reality, she's more like an appointed watchdog.

At least, that was what I thought before I met Yaana here.

At first, I thought her attitude was just an act, but after half a year, I can tell that's not the case.

She's earnest, meticulous, honest to a fault, and sometimes I catch myself pitying her a little.

"How about you, Yaana? I did a pretty good job brewing it, if I do say so myself. C'mon—don't worry. There's definitely no bugs in there or anything."

"Ugh…! No thank you!"

Strolling over boldly to sit at the table with me, his so-called master, Hyrince starts drinking his own tea without waiting for me to start first.

Meanwhile, Yaana turns red and storms out of the room after having enough of his teasing.

"Oh, some children have such short tempers."

Hyrince can't suppress a grin.

"That's not very nice."

"I can't help it; she's just so fun to tease."

I sigh as my childhood friend cackles evilly.

"There's really no need to keep provoking her, now that we know what sort of person she is…"

Originally, Hyrince teased Yaana only to gauge her temperament and feel her out.

He might seem simple and frank, but at heart, he's more thoughtful, diligent, and sincere than anything else. Not many people know this side of him.

Hyrince's usual attitude seems to come so naturally that you'd have to be incredibly observant to realize it's all a facade.

And since he's always putting on an act himself, he's gotten very good at figuring out when other people are lying or pretending.

Once Hyrince tested Yaana by deliberately provoking her multiple times, he concluded that Yaana's personality wasn't a facade, and we figured she was just being herself.

"...So why did the pontiff appoint Yaana as the saint, then?"

The position of saint is decided by appointment according to the pontiff and cardinals of the Word of God. Since the pontiff has so much sway over the Church, I'm sure he has a major say in the final decision.

If he wanted someone who would keep an eye on me, I'm sure there are other candidates better suited for that role.

I hate to say it, but I don't think Yaana is crafty enough to do that kind of thing, and I haven't seen her ever try so far, either.

"Maybe they figured it'd be preferable to not put a collar on you if they don't need to? Something along those lines?"

Hyrince sips his tea with such measured ease that it's hard to believe he's really the same age as I am.

When Hyrince isn't putting on his act, he looks incredibly mature.

The fact that he's already grown taller than most kids our age only enhances that effect.

Though to those who don't know his real nature, he probably just looks like a brawny know-it-all.

"I'm sure the pontiff doesn't really want to get on your bad side. So he probably picked a saint who would be a good ally to you. She's honest, easy to read, but still very talented. Plus, she's got a strong sense of justice, just like yours. Considering what a good match she is for you, it's actually a pretty thoughtful choice, don't you think?"

Hyrince's analysis is consistent with my own thoughts on the matter: The pontiff was likely being deeply considerate of me when he chose the saint.

Maybe he realized that I don't feel like I can trust him, and he decided to try to improve our relationship.

Yaana might be a peace offering of sorts.

"Julius, the pontiff isn't your enemy. There's no harm in being cautious of him, but if you're too paranoid, it'll only make things harder for you, you know?"

"Yeah…I guess you're right."

At Hyrince's remark, I realize that I might've been subconsciously treating the pontiff as a hostile entity.

"You're right. I can't get my foes and allies mixed up. I'm not fighting the pontiff."

I say it point by point, as if trying to convince myself.

But then Hyrince shrugs and adds, "Although that old man always makes me feel like I'm being hoodwinked."

The pontiff's gentle yet deceptive smile comes to mind.

If he knew all of this would happen and sent Yaana as a calculated move, then I'm probably playing into his hands yet again.

And I have good reason to believe that's the case, since it's happened before.

…He's not an enemy, but I still can't quite bring myself to like him.

I close the door.

Then I turn away, giving in to the feeling of helplessness for a moment.

Beyond the door at my back, the commanders sent from each nation for the task force are gathered.

With so many different nations participating, there is a great host of soldiers to manage, so each group has been dispatched with a well-known general from their respective lands.

These commanders have come here with the pride of their countries at stake.

We just finished holding a meeting with all of them.

And I'll be standing above them as the high commander.

My heart pounded with nerves at the weight and responsibility of my role as I braced myself for the meeting.

But the result was far from what I expected.

No one, not a single person, looked at me once the actual planning began.

The only time I spoke throughout the entire meeting was to introduce myself.

Then I listened to the commanders' introductions, and as soon as they started discussing specific strategies, I was pushed out of the room.

No one considered me to be in charge at all.

Not a real leader, just someone who happens to fill that post while possessing the title of Hero.

I remember how the various commanders looked at me the second I entered the room. They expected nothing from me, as if they were glancing at a pebble on the side of the road.

Nobody said anything of the sort to me, of course.

When I introduced myself, they all responded with respect.

But I could still tell, whether I wanted to or not.

To them, I'm nothing more than a figurehead.

I might be the hero, and the prince of a major kingdom, but they saw me as nothing more than a child.

Instead of shouldering the heavy weight of my role as high commander, I wasn't even given a chance. It was painfully clear that nobody wanted me to.

Beyond that door, the commanders are discussing the force's next moves.

I'm supposed to be in charge, yet I'm not even present for the discussion.

It's not as though they physically forced me out, but once they said things like *you can leave the rest to us,* it was hard to feel welcome in my seat.

Forcing the issue and staying would have accomplished nothing but lowering their appraisal of me from a reasonable figurehead to an unreasonable, troublesome child.

I have to be patient.

The commanders and I have only just met.

They have no reason to trust me yet.

Plenty of chances for that will come soon enough.

I have to close the distance between us, little by little.

There's no need to panic.

All in due time.

"It's fine. We're still only getting started."

I cling to my scarf as I try to reassure myself.

No one will hear me through that thick door.

My grip slackens, and I walk back to my room.

Then, a few days later, the task force sets out on its first expedition.

"Hey, we're heading into battle now, right?"

"Um. Yeah. I guess."

My response to Hyrince's question is slow and uncertain, but you'll have to forgive me.

I can't help but have my doubts about the situation.

This is the special task force's preliminary mission.

Since it'll be our first battle as a unit, and there's still some anxiety about how good our coordination will be, we're starting with a nearby area where the human-trafficking organization's presence is relatively low to minimize potential losses.

But even so, is this really the right thing to do?

"Feels more like a sightseeing trip than anything else."

I agree with Hyrince's candid observation, though I don't say so out loud.

We're supposed to be tracking down and defeating a covert group of traffickers...and yet, here we are in a fancy carriage.

There are knights on horseback surrounding us, as if they're supposed to guard us.

No, not "as if." That's exactly what they're doing.

Judging by our carriage alone, no one would ever guess that I'm supposed to be the in command of this entire force.

It must look more like some fancy noble or royal is coming along on vacation.

This carriage sticks out like a sore thumb, milling about in the middle of an imposing army on the march.

"There you go again!"

Sitting next to Hyrince, Yaana frowns at him.

"The commanders of the force prepared this carriage specifically for Sir Hero! To complain about it is akin to rejecting their kindness!"

She's right, of course.

And yet...

"You say that, but...do you *really* think that so-called kindness is for Julius's sake?"

At Hyrince's sharp retort, Yaana opens her mouth, then falls silent.

Seems like, deep down, she's not thrilled about this situation, either.

That's a bit of a relief.

I'm sure there are plenty of commoners who would love to ride in a carriage like this.

Hyrince and I are an upper-crust noble and royalty, respectively, even if our positions are unusual. We're used to this kind of treatment, but Yaana isn't.

From what I understand, candidates for sainthood undergo strict training from childhood and are cut off from much of the world.

If anything, I thought she might be more excited about experiencing this kind of luxury than even a commoner might be.

We haven't known each other for long, but I admit that her straightforward personality made me suspect that would be the case.

At the same time, she also has a strong sense of responsibility, so I didn't think she'd make a big fuss or anything.

Surprisingly, though, she seems to feel as uncomfortable in this situation as we do.

It turns out there are certain things you can't learn about a person without spending a good deal of time with them.

I suppose that means I have to keep communicating with others as well to get a better idea of their character and, over time, find more people I can trust.

"Um, well, you know. Maybe standing out like this will make the masses feel safer or something?"

Yaana finally squeezes out an answer, but Hyrince simply snorts.

"Commoners aren't stupid. If the point was to make people feel safe, they'd make a show of military might. You can already tell how many skilled people are in this force at a glance. I don't see any reason to put only Julius—the high commander—in a fancy carriage like this."

Considering how she doesn't attempt to raise any argument, it seems like even Yaana knows that was a feeble excuse.

"If anything, using a carriage this conspicuous runs the risk of making the people even more anxious. They'll look at it and wonder what we're really up to, if we're just traveling for sport."

Hyrince smiles grimly.

We really did get dubious looks like that as we left the town.

The activities of the human-trafficking organization aren't very widely publicized in this area.

It was natural that the townspeople who saw us setting off didn't feel any sense of urgency or danger; they watched our procession like we were holding some kind of minor festivities.

But it's not like there haven't been any kidnappings here at all.

Most of the people were only watching us leave out of curiosity, but I did see a few people looking on as if praying for our success.

And the people who wore those expressions reacted all the more strongly when they saw this carriage.

Not in a good way, either.

Anxiety, disgust, resignation—those were the feelings that flashed across the faces of the people who spotted this ostentatious thing we're riding in.

Seeing the looks on their faces made it all that much clearer how out of place the whole arrangement is.

But still...

"Even if they *were* able to see us, their reaction would probably be the same."

I'm not especially trying to agree with Yaana, but I do have a thought that conflicts slightly with Hyrince's take.

We're kids.

Hero, saint, or whatever else we might be, it doesn't change the fact that we're children.

The people who are distressed about the human-trafficking organization probably wouldn't react any better to seeing us going along with the soldiers than they did to seeing our carriage.

Because either way, we definitely don't look reliable.

"That much is true. We are kids and all. Although I still feel like there must've been a better way to do this."

Hyrince sighs and sinks deeply into his seat.

"That's not true! Even if he is a child, Sir Hero is still a striking figure! No one could look at him and feel ill at ease! Of that I'm certain!" Yaana clenches her fists earnestly as she protests. "Anyone who would fail to recognize Sir Hero's gravitas must be blind! Just look at how cool and handsome he is!"

I can't help but stare at her blankly.

Even Hyrince is so stunned that he sits there blinking, forgetting to tease her for once.

Realizing from our reactions the significance of what she's just said, Yaana turns bright red.

"P-please forget I said anything!"

She covers her face with her hands.

"Uh-*huh*..."

Recovering from his shock, Hyrince starts to smirk wickedly.

Normally, since Yaana can't contend with Hyrince in a verbal battle, she tends to flee when the tide turns against her. Unfortunately, we're currently in a carriage. There's nowhere to run.

"Waaah!"

As if trying to escape his evil clutches nonetheless, Yaana retreats to the far end of the seat and curls up in the corner.

There are no words to describe the look on Hyrince's face as he attempts to suppress his laughter.

"Wah! Eek!"

"Oof!"

Just then, the carriage bounces with a *thunk*.

Sitting in her strange position, Yaana loses her balance and almost topples out of her seat, so I hurry to catch her.

"Are you okay?"

"Y-yes, thank you..."

Yaana's face turns even redder.

Between her previous outburst and this new development, she's gone positively crimson.

Then, at the worst possible moment, the carriage door bangs open.

"...We've arrived."

The soldier who opens the door stares at us with a dreadful expression.

I can see his thoughts written clearly on his face: *Do these kids think this is a game?*

...Maybe we don't really have any right to complain about the appearance of our carriage after all.

The expedition went incredibly smoothly, at least on paper.

The members of the human-trafficking organization in this area were inferior to the task force in both skill and numbers.

Since their hideout had already been discovered beforehand, they put up very little resistance once our forces arrived and took over the place...or so I'm told.

We didn't actually get to see this with our own eyes.

We were made to wait a considerable distance away, surrounded by guards.

Not long after, our carriage returns to town.

I can hear the cheers welcoming us back, but it does nothing to lift my spirits.

To an extent, I'd expected things to be something like this, but I was still ashamed to be so blatantly treated as a purely ornamental figurehead.

I know that a child like me could never take command of a group of seasoned officers, of course.

They might be stronger than I am in combat, too, even though I'm the hero.

But still, I'm sure there must've been something I could have done.

Yet, I was forced to sit in a carriage the whole way there and back.

At this rate, there's no point in me being here at all.

Can I really go on like this?

Do I have no choice but to wait until I finally amount to something?

"Hmm? What's going on?"

As I'm lost in thought, Hyrince peers out in front of the carriage. I follow his gaze and see that we've stopped our advance.

Accordingly, our carriage slows to a halt.

"Did something happen?" Hyrince asks one of the guards.

"It would appear some of the locals have approached us."

"What, are they trying to cause trouble? Give me a break."

Hyrince grunts irritably. This first expedition must have stressed him out as well.

But I'm more concerned about the situation up ahead.

"I'll be right back."

"Huh? Hey, wait a minute!"

I open the door and jump down, heading toward the source of the commotion.

It's not long before I can make out voices.

"Did you find my daughter?!"

"Our son *is* safe, isn't he?!"

"Where are the kidnapped children?!"

Some of the townspeople crowd around the soldiers, asking for the whereabouts of the children who went missing.

But the soldiers simply exchange glances with one another and refuse to answer.

"Come on! Tell us! What happened?!"

"Where is my child? Is he safe?!"

The attitude the soldiers take seems to unnerve the locals, whose questions grow even more frantic.

Yes, the expedition to root out the local branch of the human-trafficking organization went smoothly.

At least it did on paper.

But when we broke into the hideout, the kidnapped children were nowhere to be found.

And we have no idea where they might have been taken.

Some documents were recovered from the hideout, but there's no telling if we'll get any useful information from studying them.

Looking at our returning force, it's easy to see the captured survivors of the human-trafficking organization being marched along, but it's equally obvious that the kidnapped children aren't with us.

The families of the victims, who were placing all their hopes on us, obviously want answers.

"We'll announce the details later. For now, out of the way."

One of the commanders tries to chase them off, but I quickly step in.

"Wait. Please."

"Sir Hero?"

The officer looks at me doubtfully, with an expression that contains a trace of irritation that can't be completely hidden.

In those eyes, I'm only a child who shouldn't be involving myself in this situation.

But I can't just mindlessly appease other people.

"We've taken care of all the criminals who were hiding out in this area."

I step in front of the villagers and start to speak.

Their expressions soften slightly when I announce that the organization has been eradicated from the area.

But…there's more.

I have no choice but to tell them.

"But the people who were kidnapped were no longer in their hideout when we arrived."

Even if we staved them off here, they would've found out soon enough.

"No…"

"Does that mean…you were…too late…?"

Silence. And then…

"Damn you!"

"How could you do this?! Answer me!"

Outrage.

The villagers surge forward as if to strike me, and the soldiers scramble to hold them back.

"Sir Hero, what have you done?!"

The commander grabs my shoulder, looking frustrated at my insolence.

But I shake off the hand.

At the same time, one woman breaks through the wall of soldiers and rushes up to me.

The commander tries to step in front of me immediately, but I raise a hand to let her through.

With tears in her eyes, the woman brings her palm down to strike me.

But I catch her hand before the blow lands.

"I'm afraid we didn't get there in time."

I can't let her hit me, even if I sympathize.

Once, back in the ruins of Keren County in Sariella, I allowed the survivors to take out their anger on me, making no attempt to resist their violence.

But Mr. Tiva admonished me for that.

Hitting me would only make them feel better for a few moments.

Soon enough, their hands would hurt, and their hearts would ache from the guilt.

The person who throws the punch and the person who receives it are both left with only pain.

Mr. Tiva explained to me then that it's important not to let people hit me at times like these.

"We will continue to chase down the organization. I cannot promise you that we'll find those who were kidnapped. But I can at least promise you that we will never give up."

I can't make vows lightly.

For all we know, it could very well already be too late to save the victims.

But we must do everything in our power until the moment their fates become clear.

That much I can promise.

I let go of the woman's hand, and she breaks down sobbing.

Building up my reputation, feeling frustrated over my uselessness... How could I have gotten hung up on such useless ideas?

What am I?

I'm a hero.

And it's a hero's job to help people who are suffering!

I can't believe I forgot the most important thing of all.

I don't know if my words satisfied any of them.

But the townspeople slowly withdraw from the road, their anger retreating.

Even the woman who had fallen to her knees weeping stands up and shuffles away.

And as she does so, she murmurs, "I'm sorry."

Mr. Tiva was right. I made the correct choice.

"Sir Hero, we cannot have you simply doing as you please."

Once things calm down, the commander starts to scold me.

"There is no reason for you to face the anger of the public."

"That's not true," I respond simply. "I am the high commander of this expedition. I have a responsibility to hear them out. Even if I am just a figurehead, I am still in charge."

At that, the officer sucks in a breath.

"We didn't make it in time. Yes, since we broke up the hideout, the threat here has been eliminated. But we weren't able to undo what has already been done. That is reality."

"But our duty is not—"

"Yes, strictly speaking, that is not our duty. But even so...we failed."

Even if it's not our fault, we can't forget that we didn't do what was expected of us.

If we had, we might have been able to save them.

But we didn't.

And we must never forget that reality, no matter what.

"I know I haven't done anything, nor is there anything I could have done. I know this is all merely lip service. But if I can't even make promises like that, then I'm not fit to be the hero."

With that, I turn my back on the commander and return to our carriage.

Once inside, Hyrince kindly greets me with a *what am I going to do with you* sort of smile.

At times like these, I'm grateful to have a friend who understands me without a word needing to be said.

Although I'm not sure why Yaana is fidgeting bashfully next to him.

"Hyrince. I'm going to do it."

"Of course. I'll be right behind you."

Hyrince doesn't ask me *do what?* or anything like that.

He simply says that he'll follow me, no matter what I'm planning.

Yes, I still have plenty of time.

I thought I could slowly get closer to the members of the force, little by little.

But that's not good enough.

I might have time, but with every second that passes, there are people who can no longer be saved.

They don't have a single moment to spare.

Why does a hero fight?

For the people.

I finally remember that resolution I made.

And so I can't afford to take my time.

With renewed determination, I keep moving forward.

Special Chapter   THE EMPIRE VETERAN AND THE COMMANDER

"I heard there was an incident."

"Ah, Sir Tiva. Yes, you could say that."

The commander in question looks away evasively.

As the deputy high commander, I'm technically ranked above him, but he's a man of no small importance in his own country, so it seems his pride prevents him from completely deferring to me as his superior officer.

All the more so with Sir Hero, who is so much younger than he is.

And this man isn't the only commander who feels that way.

Those who were invited to be commanders in the special task force all boast individual strength and a long list of accomplishments, so they're unsurprisingly reluctant to serve under a child with no experience, even if he is the hero.

Which is why they reached the unspoken agreement of treating Sir Hero as no more than a figurehead.

I cannot say that choice is entirely wrong.

Sir Hero is a child, and admittedly one without any deeds to his name.

It's only logical to assume that it would be more effective for the commanders with experience to lead the force with their knowledge.

If you ignore the temperament of the hero, that is.

"What does Sir Hero look like to you?"

At that, the commander appears to think carefully.

He must be trying to figure out the correct way to answer my question.

"No need to overthink it. You can just tell me what you really think. I swear to you that I will tell no one."

Since the commanders come from so many different countries, the force is a jumble of different motivations and interests.

One wrong word from any of them could put their country at a disadvantage.

I assume that is why this man is reluctant to give me his frank opinion.

He hesitates a moment longer, then utters one short sentence:

"I think he may be a little bit too direct."

But I'm sure it isn't simply my imagination when I sense that there are many complex feelings contained in his words.

No doubt, he resents Sir Hero for escalating the conflict with the townspeople.

But is there not perhaps some small part of him that admires the boy's dazzling sincerity?

"Sir Hero is a child, so we adults must set a proper example for him."

"Of course."

"At least, I'm sure that's the false impression most of the force is laboring under."

"Eh?"

The man nods along at first but then blinks in surprise at the last part of my statement.

"The title of Hero is bestowed upon the person who the gods deem most fitting for the role," I say, though that much is common knowledge to everyone. "So yes, Sir Hero is a child. But he was selected as the hero over any of us adults. I think it might be prudent for all of us to think long and hard about what that means."

The commander falls into stunned silence.

All the commanders in this force are people of great importance.

But none of them was chosen to be the hero.

Instead, the title was given to Sir Julius, who is still yet a child.

Does that mean we adults were all deemed unfit?

Or that Sir Hero is simply more exceptional than any of us?

I'm sure the commanders will all learn the answer soon enough. I've already seen it for myself.

I witnessed his incredibly noble spirit in the former Keren County of Sariella, regardless of his age.

The title is not what makes him the hero.

He is the hero because he is already worthy.

He won't allow the commanders to continue treating him as a useless figurehead forever, whatever they might think.

I'm sure he'll break through that wall soon enough.

And I imagine when the time comes, he will grow all the better for it.

I need only look on, as much as I may wish to interfere.

Partly because I believe that he must be able to confront this level of adversity on his own.

But also because the commanders must learn what kind of a person Sir Hero truly is.

My meddling would be of no help to him here.

"May I ask what it is you fight for?"

"Me...?"

The commander looks uncertain, avoiding my gaze.

"As you grow older, you begin to forget what it is you're fighting for. For your nation, for the people, or perhaps for yourself? There are many reasons, but no doubt in the beginning, you fought for one of them with great passion."

To fight means to constantly risk death.

Without dedication, few would ever be able to overcome that horror and fight.

But as one continues to fight, that passion slowly turns into force of habit, and you begin to forget your reasons for being on the battlefield.

"Sir Hero would be able to answer right away, I am sure."

That's why he shines so brilliantly in the eyes of his elders, like me.

"You said he is too direct, but is that really such a problem? Are heroes not exactly the kind of people who can face problems head-on and stay true to a creed?"

The commander falls silent, unable to respond to my question.

But that reaction is answer enough.

Sophia's Diary 2

I've been sent off to the academy.

A boarding school.

How dare they do such a thing!

I already scarcely ever got to see Merazophis, and now I have to stay at a boarding school?!

And we're not even allowed to leave without submitting a request?

There are formalities involved in having visitors at the academy, too?

But that'll just make it even harder for me to go see Merazophis or for him to come see me!

How dare they!

How DARE they!

Well, clearly I've got no choice but to run away!

But when I tried to break my dorm window and rush straight to Merazophis, I somehow found myself tied up in thread an instant later.

I could barely move, but I managed to turn my head in time to see Sael, Riel, and Fiel high-fiving.

Are they here just to keep an eye on me?!

Honestly, how DARE they!

J3 JULIUS, AGE 12: SURPRISE ATTACK

It's all well and good to make grand resolutions, but what follows is a series of small steps.

First, I tried participating in the strategy meetings to open up a dialogue with the commanders, but to little avail.

Since I'd forced my way into participating, everyone pretended I wasn't present.

They were discussing where the force should head next and what strategy they should use to track down and dismantle the organization's presence there.

There was very little I could add to that conversation. I didn't want to say pointless things and get in the way.

I had no input on what our next destination should be, since that involved many political factors, and I never found any fault with the strategy drafted by the experienced commanders.

Ultimately, I usually just sit in on the meetings in silence.

…I'd like to think that even showing my face at the meetings has purpose.

And as expected, I had no part to play on the field, either.

Since the human-trafficking organization operates across so many different nations, its total scale is undeniably enormous.

However, that holds true only when looking at the big picture.

In terms of the small individual branches in each area, they're hardly any different from your run-of-the-mill band of thieves.

In fact, it seems like the human-trafficking organization more often than not uses whatever active criminals they find in their target regions and simply folds them into their nefarious schemes.

Since these outlaws usually skulk outside the safety of towns in places where monsters also lurk, they're fairly strong.

But the special task force consists of elite soldiers drawn from every nation. Of course they're not going to lose to bandits.

No matter how many levels the brigands have, they can't match fighters who have formal training and combat experience.

Our force's commanders thoroughly research the makeup of each local branch of the organization and then devise an appropriate strategy before raiding the hideouts, meaning the criminals don't stand a chance.

And there's no place for me in this efficient process of steadily crushing the organization.

That's fine, of course. I'm glad that it's going well.

And yet...

"Am I really even necessary?"

"That's way too deep a question for me to answer."

Hyrince shakes his head at my musing.

"*Hiyah!*"

With a loud cry, a wooden sword comes hurtling down at my head.

I quickly raise my own wooden sword to parry it.

I'm currently doing some independent training.

As a figurehead commander, I have plenty of time to spare, so Hyrince and I have been doing some sparring.

Of course, Hyrince can't beat me, thanks to my Hero title.

Our level of technique is around the same, but the difference in our stats makes me much stronger.

"*Tch!*"

Seeing his big swing foiled, Hyrince clicks his tongue and quickly jumps back.

But before he can fully retreat, I close in on him and swing my sword from one side to the other.

Hyrince blocks the practice sword with a wooden shield.

Realizing early on that he would never beat me blow for blow, Hyrince quickly abandoned a sword-focused style and instead opted for a shield in one hand and his sword in the other.

He's got a better constitution than most people our age, so he's strong enough to wield both effectively, even with only one hand for each.

Attacking with a powerful swing of his sword and defending with a sturdy shield he keeps raised.

His stable fighting style reflects his personality perfectly.

Ever since he started using a shield, his results have definitely improved in our sparring matches.

"Owww. Ugh, okay, I surrender."

In that it takes more time for him to surrender, that is.

No matter how well he might fight, it's not enough to make up for the differences in our stats.

Even after intercepting my attack with his shield, Hyrince was still sent flying.

Plus, that move left a huge crack in his wooden shield.

"Aw, man. I'm gonna have to replace this thing."

Hyrince sighs as he looks at his ruined shield.

"Sorry."

"It's fine, it's fine. Practice or not, you won't get much out of it if you hold back, right?"

"That's true."

I really have learned a lot from these sparring matches.

To be honest, I'm not particularly good with a sword.

My mentor, Master Ronandt, is a legendary mage, so I'm more adept with magic than weapons.

I wound up separated from him by the Word of God Church due to his radical training methods.

But in the short time we spent together, my magic abilities made a huge leap forward.

That man really is amazing...even if he does have some serious issues.

At any rate, with these sparring matches, I can try to bring my swordsmanship up to par with my magic.

There are a lot of things that can be learned only by crossing swords with another person, things I'd never figure out by practicing on my own.

Even if my stats are higher than Hyrince's, our abilities and skills aren't too far apart.

That's how we've been pushing each other to greater heights.

If anything, I think continuously challenging someone with higher stats like me is helping Hyrince hone his skills even faster.

Then the sound of clapping brings me out of my thoughts.

Turning around, I see that Mr. Tiva has been watching us.

"Bravo. Excellent work. I'm impressed that you can move like that at such a young age."

"Thank you very much. But I'm sure I still couldn't come close to being a match for you, right?"

I thank him for the praise, but I'm fairly certain my swordsmanship still can't hold a candle to his.

"Heh. I suppose not. Believe it or not, I was once said to be second in skill only to the prior sword-king, the so-called god of swordsmanship himself. These old bones won't lose to a youngster like you just yet."

No wonder Mr. Tiva is a general of the empire.

The previous sword-king was considered on par with Master Ronandt in power.

If he was second only to a man on the same level as my insanely powerful master, Mr. Tiva really is no ordinary person—not that I didn't already suspect as much.

"But of course, that's only in terms of swordsmanship. You've been trained in magic by Sir Ronandt. If anything, magic is your primary weapon more than your sword. If you combine the two, you might even be able to land a hit or two on me."

"I notice you didn't say I might beat you."

"Ha-ha. Old as I may be, I do have my pride. I can hardly go around losing to youngsters barely older than my grandson."

Mr. Tiva looks over at Hyrince, who's stepped away in silence to avoid intruding on our conversation.

"Your name is Hyrince, correct?"

"Yes, sir."

"Let me see that a moment."

Tiva borrows the cracked wooden shield from Hyrince.

"Sir Hero, please attack me with all your might."

As I look at him uncertainly, Mr. Tiva holds the shield in his left hand.

"What? But…"

"It's all right."

I'm worried about what might happen if I hit that cracked shield as hard as I can, but he smiles reassuringly.

"All right, then."

I decide to trust him and swing my wooden sword with all my strength.

The sword comes down on the shield from above, but just as it makes contact—I feel something strange.

The next thing I know, I'm holding the sword out to the side at a strange angle.

"What was that?"

"I deflected your attack," Tiva explains. "Instead of trying to bear the brunt of its power, I simply changed its direction."

Tiva hands the shield back to Hyrince.

"If your opponent is too strong, you won't accomplish much by trying to block their attacks head-on. At times, you must create an opening by re-directing their strength. Those who wield shields are often in danger because of this. Quick decisions need to be made about which attacks can be blocked or deflected. You have a fine eye and a quick mind. No doubt you will make a great shield bearer one day."

"Thank you. That's very helpful."

Tiva claps Hyrince on the shoulder encouragingly.

"I must say, I'm almost envious. The Analeit Kingdom has many promising youngsters, not only Sir Hero here."

With that, Mr. Tiva departs from the training grounds.

"Huh. He complimented me. I'm just your attendant, though."

"What's wrong with that? You can be my guard, too."

Besides, this friend is more than just an attendant to me.

Even putting aside my bias, Hyrince is undeniably talented, and I'm sure he doesn't want to be a mere attendant forever, either.

If he did, he wouldn't be sparring with me like this.

I'm sure Hyrince wants to fight by my side, not just follow along behind me.

Or am I being vain?

Once again, we're rocking back and forth inside a carriage.

Fortunately, I was at least able to convince the commanders to switch out the fancy carriage for a standard military transport.

But that's just about the only change; I still get shoved into a carriage and don't get to do anything during our expeditions.

This time will be the same...or at least, that's what I thought.

Suddenly, I hear a commotion outside the cart.

At the same time, I can hear several impacts.

"What's happening?"

"Yaana! Don't go near the window!"

The girl saint tries to peer outside, but I grab her shoulder and pull her back.

Seconds later, an arrowhead crashes into the window.

"Eek?!"

The arrow doesn't break the window, embedding itself partway into the glass.

But if Yaana had poked her head out, she could've been hit.

"An attack—must be an ambush." Hyrince groans.

Outside the carriage, I hear the shouts and clanging of soldiers trying to fend off the rain of arrows.

The quiet *thunk-thunk* of them impacting the wood encasing us continues, so there must be a considerable amount coming at us.

Fortunately, since we switched to a sturdy military carriage, arrows don't have much effect.

If they can't even break through the glass, we should be safe in the cabin.

As long as the enemy only has arrows, at least.

But even if we're safe inside the carriage, the same isn't true of the soldiers outside.

"Yaana, you stay in here! Hyrince, protect her!"

"Julius—dammit! All right."

Hyrince starts to object but changes his mind when he sees Yaana's face, pale from the attack.

"Huh? What? Sir Hero, what about you?"

"Don't worry. Just trust me."

I smile as gently as I can to reassure the anxious Yaana.

Then I gather my courage and leap out of the carriage, quickly shutting the door behind me.

Noticing me, the soldiers guarding our carriage stare with wide eyes.

"Sir Hero?! It's too dangerous! Go back inside at once!"

"We'll protect you—don't worry!"

Immediately, several guards rush over and raise their shields around me, trying to usher me back into the carriage.

In this moment, I'm not only a figurehead commander to them but also a vulnerable child and even a burden.

An object to be protected, since it would be troublesome if I died.

But that's not how it should be. That's not right at all!

"Don't worry about me! Protect the wounded!" I shout.

At the same time, I create a light barrier with magic.

It doesn't have the sturdiness that the physical mass an Earth Magic barrier would provide, but it should be enough to stop arrows that can't penetrate a glass window.

"Who am I?!" I raise my voice so everyone around me can hear. "I am the hero! And is the hero someone to be protected?! No! The hero is someone who protects others!"

Even as I shout, enemy arrows keep raining down.

But all of them are blocked by my barrier before they reach us.

"Don't be afraid! These missiles have little force behind them! As long as they don't hit a vital spot, they won't kill us!"

I push the soldiers aside as they try to protect me, making my way to the front.

The arrows are coming from a forest on the side of the road.

Judging by the amount of arrows, I'd estimate the archers number in the dozens.

Certainly less than a hundred, but not exactly a small amount, either.

If I remember right, that should be the full strength of the human-trafficking organization in this area.

In other words, they must have brought all their members to lie in wait and ambush us here.

The human traffickers aren't stupid. It's only natural that they would take countermeasures if they found out we're going after them.

We haven't been making any real effort to hide our activities, after all.

We've been traveling through towns, mostly to reassure the people there.

So it makes sense that we'd run into an ambush or two.

In fact, it's almost been going *too* well until now.

But the soldiers of the task force must have gotten too used to things going well, or perhaps the chain of command is still in disarray because they're a mishmash of so many different nations. Either way, the unit's reaction is far too slow and uncertain.

"Move the wounded back to safety! Soldiers with shields, to the front!"

At a glance, there don't seem to be any fatalities yet, but I can definitely spot some soldiers with arrows piercing their arms or legs.

That's why I give the order to evacuate the wounded and command the shield bearers to assemble on the front lines.

But it's not happening fast enough.

The soldiers each look at their respective commanders questioningly, and they start moving only after the commanders nod.

We're still under attack. Why aren't they moving faster?

In our battles so far, they've executed prearranged plans to great success, so this is the first time they've had to react on the spot.

Now it's all too clear that the chain of command hasn't been properly defined.

Maybe they're not hurrying because we're not in too much trouble yet.

The arrows flying at us aren't particularly powerful. And the task force is composed of elite soldiers, so this isn't that impressive of an attack to them.

Most of the wounded were hit only in the initial surprise attack.

Now that we're past that, there's hardly any concern of the arrows claiming lives.

But as a result, they're calm enough to look to their commanders for confirmation instead of just following my orders.

If we were in a real pinch right now, maybe they would've obeyed me without question.

I'm glad there's no threat of further casualties, of course, but it's frustrating that the men won't react quickly enough.

We can't just defend ourselves forever, after all.

Our goal is to eliminate the human-trafficking organization, so we have to defeat whoever's attacking us right now.

If we can just weather this attack, the odds will most likely work out in our favor.

The bandits don't have an endless supply of arrows, so once they run out, we can go on the offensive.

But will they stand around waiting for us to reach them?

No, I doubt it.

If they're smart enough to lie in wait and ambush us, I'm sure they'll recognize when it would be in their best interest to flee.

And if they run away, that doesn't mean we've won—quite the opposite.

Any of them who get away will simply go on to commit the same crimes in other areas.

Letting any escape runs counter to all the reasons why we've come here in the first place.

"Those who are able, follow me!"

I draw my sword and dash toward the forest.

Arrows slice through the air around me as I rush out on my own, but I block the barrage with my barrier without slowing down.

Before long, I reach the tree line.

The ambushers hidden in the trees cast aside their bows and draw their swords.

Their collective faces seem a little stressed but far from panicked. Probably because they've noticed I'm a child. They've lowered their guard.

It's not only my allies who take me lightly because of my age.

Enemies are actually all the more likely to underestimate me because of my appearance.

Fine by me!

"Hiyaaah!"

One bandit slashes at me with a sword, but I repel it.

The unimpressive arrow barrage has given me a rough idea of our enemy's strength.

Even if we trade blows head-on, I'll clearly come out on top.

I knock back the sword with my own, and it falls from the man's hand, clattering away behind him.

"Huh?"

The man looks blankly at his now-empty sword hand.

He's wide open.

But I...

"Ah!"

...I hesitate for only a moment.

Then I cut the outlaw down.

I feel my sword sink into his flesh.

That's enough confirmation to know that I've at least incapacitated him, so I move on to the next enemy without looking to see the result.

...No, that's only an excuse.

I'm simply afraid to see what I just did.

Afraid to come to terms with the reality that I slew someone.

I'm too inexperienced a fighter to incapacitate someone without killing them.

So I had no other choice.

...For the first time in my life, I killed someone with my own hands.

"...ro! Sir Hero!"

"Huh?"

Mr. Tiva shakes me by the shoulders, bringing me back to my senses.

"It's all right now. The enemy's been wiped out."

Blinking, I realize he's right, although I don't know how it happened.

My memories of the rest of the battle after I cut down that one man are hazy.

I think I was fighting in a trance.

Just like that other time.

The first battlefield I ever experienced.

The day I fought the Nightmare of the Labyrinth.

That time, I was terrified as the Nightmare slaughtered people one after another, but I still stepped forward despite myself.

The horror of facing down such an impossibly strong opponent was so great that I barely remember that moment.

I found myself jumping in front of the Nightmare of the Labyrinth, and next thing I knew, it was all over.

And the battle after that went much the same way.

When the swarm of spiders attacked that town of Keren County, I lost myself in the fighting, and by the time I came to my senses, my master had already won.

How shameful.

From the looks of things, I haven't grown a bit since then.

I've trained so much and improved on my stats and skills.

But that doesn't matter if I can't keep my cool on the battlefield.

I inhale deeply and let out the breath slowly.

Somehow, that seems to bring my vision back to normal.

I start to see things I couldn't a moment ago and hear things that were deafened.

The bandits lying prone all over the ground.

My allies inspecting the bodies.

The sound of a commander barking orders.

Everything is a confirmation that the battle has indeed ended.

"It's...all over."

"Yes, that's right."

I was only speaking to myself, but another voice responds.

Turning around, I see Mr. Tiva standing there with a grave expression.

...In fact, his hand is still on my shoulder.

If I didn't even realize that, I guess I must still be more shaken up than I thought.

I take another deep breath.

As I do so, the thick stench of blood assails my nose and mouth, causing me to choke.

It's not that I've never smelled blood before, but certainly not enough times to be used to it yet.

And this is the first time that I've been the source of it.

I cough a few times, then breathe deeply again once I've settled down.

This time, I do my best to ignore the smell of blood.

"Feeling a little calmer?"

"Yes, thank you."

Mr. Tiva gently removes his hand from my shoulder.

I'm still clutching my sword in both hands, so I try to put it back in its scabbard, but my left hand won't let go of the hilt.

"Huh?"

I try again, but I'm shaking too much.

After a great deal of effort, I manage to wrench my hand free, but my movements are as stiff and shaky as if I've been caught in a snowstorm.

Getting my sword back into its scabbard still proves difficult, as the clots of blood stuck to it are in the way.

I should probably clean it off somehow before putting it away, but I can't bring myself to do it right now. I'll have to take care of it later when I've calmed down.

"The others can handle the rest. Please, Sir Hero, go back to your carriage for now."

"Right. Yes. I'll do that."

I nod slowly at Tiva's offer.

There's still a lot to do: apprehending the surviving criminals, treating our wounded allies, and so on.

But in my current state, I'd only be in the way.

I start walking toward the carriage, and Tiva falls into step beside me. After a moment, he asks a question.

"…Why did you run out on your own?"

"I thought it was the right thing to do."

At the time, I was the only one who moved quickly.

So the most logical decision was for me to take action so the enemy wouldn't get away.

"Even though you've clearly pushed yourself past your limits?"

At that, I can't help but fall silent.

Even now, I don't think my decision was wrong.

If I hadn't moved right then, some of the criminals would've gotten away.

There's little doubt about that.

And I knew I could exterminate the attackers, so I did just that.

In practical terms, I'm confident that I made the best decision.

But I didn't take my own emotional fragility into account.

"I'm so ashamed."

I clench my trembling fist.

I was able to defeat them easily.

So why am I in such a pitiful state now?

I thought I knew that fighting a human-trafficking organization would mean fighting other humans. I thought I was ready for that.

Yet, when it comes down to it, this is the result.

Pathetic.

There's no excuse!

"Sir Hero…" Mr. Tiva kneels down to match my eye level. "Please know that there's no need to push yourself so. That's why you have all of us."

I can tell from his words and demeanor that Mr. Tiva is truly worried about me.

But still…

"Or are we not reliable enough?"

"……"

Mr. Tiva looks right into my eyes, and I turn my head away.

I know that's more than enough of an answer in itself, but there's nothing else I can do right now.

Instead, I quickly move away and walk toward the carriage.

This time, Tiva doesn't chase after me, but I hear him mutter something in a quiet yet forceful voice.

"…Cowardly!"

I don't know who that was directed toward.

But I know he's not saying it about me.

I can tell that much, yet it still feels as if he's berating my weakness, and it's almost too much to bear.

"Hey. Good work out there."

As I return to the carriage, Hyrince greets me.

He's holding several arrows, probably in the process of pulling them out of the carriage.

"Get in and sit down, okay?"

"Uh-huh."

Hyrince opens the door, and I obediently go inside and take a seat.

Immediately, the exhaustion hits me all at once.

Physically, of course, but emotionally even more so.

I know I should always conduct myself like a royal and a hero, but I can't help slumping into an unseemly posture.

Fortunately, there's no one around to see but Hyrince.

Then I realize there should be one other person here.

"Where's Yaana?"

"She's healing the soldiers. Don't worry about her—you can just rest."

Before I can think that I should be working, too, Hyrince cuts me off.

"All right."

I take him up on his offer and sink deep into the carriage seat.

Special Chapter   THE SAINT AND THE EMPIRE VETERAN

"Yaana, why did they pick you?"

When I was chosen as the saint, that was the first thing one of my fellow saint candidates and close friends said to me.

I'd been elated about the unexpected offer, but those words brought down my mood right away.

Candidates for sainthood are trained from a young age.

Many girls withdraw before the end, unable to bear the severe training.

It's a difficult life, but we keep at it in hopes of becoming the future saint, all so we can someday support the hero.

Naturally, being chosen as the saint is the ultimate honor for us.

Only one person can be chosen, of course.

And even then, a new saint can be chosen only when a new hero is born.

Customarily, the chosen candidate is one who's close in age to the hero, so even the most exceptional candidate usually won't be chosen if she's not the right age.

The vast majority of candidates will never become saints.

But there's no telling when a hero might pass on and a new saint might be needed, so new trainees are still initiated every year.

In order to have a tiny chance of becoming a saint.

And I was chosen for the role.

It was as if fortune had smiled on me.

Naturally, I was so thrilled and excited that I ran to tell my good friend.

She was older than I was but always treated me kindly, so I was sure she'd be happy for me.

But as soon as she spoke, I realized I was wrong.

"Ah—I'm sorry. I didn't mean it like that…"

She apologized right away, apparently regretting her choice of words.

But then she seemed to have nothing else to say. She just hung her head, turned around, and hurried away.

My friend was two years older than I was.

Sir Julius, the new hero, is the same age as I am.

If the candidate chosen has to be close to the hero's age, surely she was qualified, too, being only two years apart.

I, on the other hand, couldn't think of any reason I'd be chosen except for my age.

My aptitudes weren't bad; they were above average certainly.

But there were other candidates who ranked better than I did, including my friend.

So although I'd always done my best, I didn't think I'd ever be chosen as the saint.

Depending on their grades, an unselected candidate for sainthood can still get a good job.

If anything, that was what I was aiming for.

I dreamed of being the saint, of course, but I thought that realistically, there was no way I'd really become the saint.

So I didn't fully understand the weight of taking on that role.

I didn't realize that becoming the saint meant trampling on the hopes of all the others who weren't chosen.

The girls who tried to be the saint and failed.

For their sakes, I have to carry on their hopes and become the best saint I can be.

So that no one will ask me "*Why?*" ever again.

Since I never really expected to become the saint, I'm sure there are other candidates who would scoff at me for making this resolution so late in the game.

But once I've made up my mind, I never go back on my word.

I have to become the kind of saint who those candidates can never find fault with.

Half of that is out of a sense of duty.

The other half…is fear.

Once the saint has been appointed, there are only three ways the title can pass on to someone new.

One is if the current hero, Sir Julius, passes away.

The other two ways are if I become unable to fulfill my role as the saint.

In other words, if I become unable to heal due to a serious illness or injury or if I die.

There are very few instances of a saint being assassinated by a candidate for sainthood.

We're taught to be noble and virtuous during our training, so there are few who would ever think of doing such a thing.

But that doesn't mean there are none at all.

I don't want to believe that my former fellow candidates and friends would even consider doing something like that to me, but I know some of them are displeased.

After all, even my closest friend reacted that way.

"Urgh!"

"Lady Saint, please don't force yourself."

I try and fail to hold back the bile that rises unbidden in my throat at the scene before me.

And the stench.

Blood, guts, and the distinct smell of body odor. The bandits who lived outside the town must've had poor hygiene practices, for the natural stench of their bodies is horrible.

It wouldn't be so bad if it was only the stench of blood—I've experienced that in the hands-on medical training I went through while being trained as a candidate for sainthood by the Church.

At first, the smell of blood bothered me, but I got used to it after experiencing it several times.

But that was from patients in a sanitary hospital ward, not victims on a real battlefield.

Here, there are other odors mixed in with the blood, along with dirt and dust of battle.

All of it combined assails me with nausea far worse than any I experienced in training.

"It's all right. I can't be faint of heart after Sir Hero fought so valiantly."

Gently rejecting the soldier who tried to guide me back to the carriage, I request instead that he lead me to the wounded to begin treating them.

Once I start healing, I'm able to focus on that alone, instead of being affected by my surroundings.

For better or worse, I've yet to be called on to do anything, since the anti-human-trafficking force was first formed.

There are proper doctors and healers in the party, and things have been going almost too smoothly thus far, so I haven't been brought out to heal.

Even this time, nobody asked for my help.

But after seeing Sir Hero take it upon himself to dive into the fray, I can't just sit on the sidelines doing nothing.

"Next!"

"Lady Saint, the majority of the wounded have already been healed."

Indeed, I look around and notice that there aren't any more soldiers with serious wounds.

"What about the captured criminals, then?"

The only victims gathered here are the soldiers, so the captives must be someplace else.

They fought against Sir Hero and company, so surely, they're gravely wounded as well.

"...Most of the criminals have breathed their last. No healing will be necessary."

"I...I see."

From the soldier's hesitation, I can tell that most of the criminals must have met a gruesome end.

"It would have been better if only Sir Hero had captured some of them alive for us..."

The soldier seems to assume that I'm grieving for the dead criminals, and he murmurs something that sounds like a criticism of Sir Hero.

"No, that's not true."

...To be honest, I was afraid to see Sir Hero fighting.

My private impression of him is an incredibly kind boy of the same age as me.

He's always smiling amiably and seems so warm that one might wonder if he could even hurt a fly. I confess, though it's disrespectful, that I doubted whether he could really fight.

But he has a strong sense of duty, and watching him work hard to earn the respect of the adults only deepened my fondness for him.

He's struggling with a weighty role, just like me, I thought.

But I was wrong.

It's more than his position or sense of duty that makes Sir Hero work hard: It's his strong desire for justice.

"Sir Hero didn't have time to worry about such things. If he let them get away, they would have scattered to other areas, and we would've lost the chance to take them all out at once. And then they would have continued to commit terrible crimes in other places, even if only on a smaller scale. Sir Hero realized this and decided that they had to be wiped out before that could happen, even if it meant doing the deed himself."

In battle, Sir Hero fought with a bloodcurdling intensity that was a far cry from his usual kind self.

His downright merciless fighting style showed how determined he was to stop the criminals at all costs.

"What? No, no…surely, Sir Hero didn't think about all that?"

"It looked that way to me."

"But even if some got away, the harm done would be negligible…"

"Would you still say the same if the victims were your own family?"

At that last comment, the soldier's excuses fall away.

"Admittedly, the people who live in this area are strangers to us for the most part. But Sir Hero pushed himself beyond his limits to protect those very same strangers."

While I was healing the wounded, I overheard soldiers who were displeased that Sir Hero had taken matters into his own hands.

They said he was being reckless because he wanted more accomplishments to his name.

That he has no sense of teamwork because he's a child.

That because the person they're supposed to be protecting charged into battle, they were forced to charge into battle as well, and so on.

It's true that acting on his own wasn't exactly commendable.

But he was motivated by a desire to protect the people, a sense of justice deeper than anyone knows.

"Exactly."

Turning around, I see the deputy high commander Sir Tiva walking over to us.

His voice, far more strained and emotional than usual, takes me by surprise.

"Sir Tiva, your hand is bleeding!"

Noticing blood dripping from his tightly clenched fist, I rush over to heal him, but he holds me off.

"It's all right. I must not heal this wound, as a reminder to myself."

Sir Tiva opens his hand and gazes at the wound, then clenches it shut again.

"I am ashamed of my cowardliness," he says quietly. "Forcing Sir Hero to push himself this far… I am a failure as his deputy."

"…Sir Hero is a child. Is it not a child's job to push past their limits?"

One of the soldiers, probably a commander based on his attire, attempts to comfort Mr. Tiva but is met with a shout of rage.

"And what does that make us, if even a child doesn't think he can rely on us?! Sir Hero was forced into action because we were too craven!"

The commander's attempt to soothe Mr. Tiva instead sets off an explosion he was holding back.

"I thought we could let Sir Hero grow up at his own pace, that he would slowly close the distance between himself and the troops. But it seems we are the ones who still have growing to do."

The commander looks away as Tiva continues.

"We've forgotten why this force exists in the first place. Our goal is to protect as many innocent victims from this organization as we can! Sir Hero understood that better than any of us. We've all been utter fools!"

Mr. Tiva's voice echoes around the vicinity.

I'm sure the rest of the soldiers heard him, too.

I don't think things will change right away.

But I have the feeling this might be the start of something new.

"Hey, welcome back."

When I return to the carriage, Sir Hero's attendant, Hyrince, waves to me. He's rather rude, so I admit I'm not very fond of him.

"Where's Sir Hero?"

Hyrince points silently into the carriage.

Peering through the window, I see Sir Hero fast asleep in his seat.

In this moment, he looks like nothing more than an innocent young boy.

But this is the hero, the one and only savior chosen by the gods.

"Julius really worked hard today, so he's exhausted. Let the guy sleep for now, will ya?"

"Not this again. I know you are Sir Hero's childhood friend, but you must refer to him with more respect!"

Sir Hero is worthy of the utmost respect.

I realized that all over again today.

And yet, this insolent boy takes him far too lightly!

"I dunno. If anything, maybe *you* should stop calling him 'Sir Hero,' yeah?"

"What are you talking about? Enough with your jokes."

I scoff at Hyrince.

How can he spout such foolishness?

"I wasn't really joking, though. You guys are gonna be together forever, right? Not in the marriage sense, though."

"F-f-f-forever?! M-m-m-m-marriage?!"

Now that he mentions it...!

Sir Hero and...me?

As I picture the two of us close to each other, my face flushes red.

Since I was raised among women at the sainthood candidate training school, I'm not used to that sort of thing.

"...I literally said it wouldn't be like that, but whatever." Hyrince sighs for some reason. "It *is* true that the hero and saint keep their roles their whole lives. You'll be together until one of you dies."

As I huff at him, Hyrince responds in an unexpectedly serious tone.

"Do you plan on staying so formal with him forever?"

"Well..."

Now that he's pointed it out, I realize that maybe I have been overly distant toward the hero.

"I'm not saying you have to be best buddies or try to force a super-close relationship or anything. I just think you might want to reconsider calling him 'Sir Hero' and stuff. Makes it seem like there's a wall between you."

"A wall…"

I was merely trying to express my respect by calling him "Sir Hero." But is that how he feels about our relationship as well?

"Well, I'm not gonna force ya. But if it were me, I wouldn't call him by his title at all. Makes it seem like you're not seeing the real Julius, just his title."

"The real…him…"

Am I truly seeing the real Sir Hero…no, Sir Julius?

Or have I been seeing him through the lens of his title?

Suddenly, I'm not sure.

"As much as it irks me to take your advice…I'll think about it."

"Sounds good."

Normally, Hyrince would be sure to tease me over this, but this time, he smiles as gently and warmly as Sir Julius.

YAANA

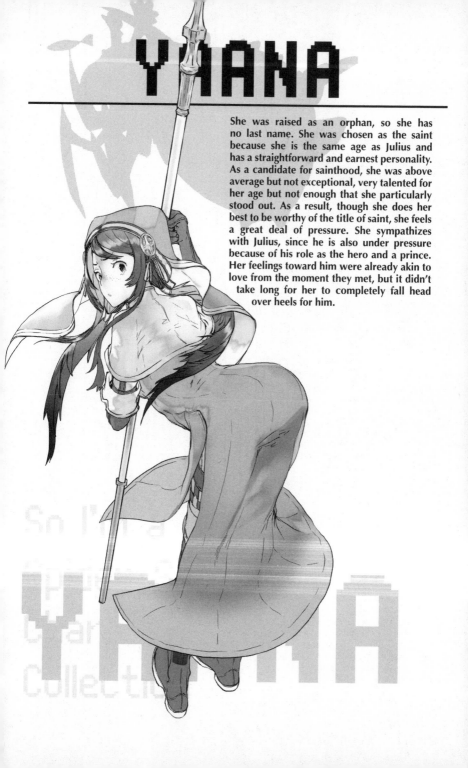

She was raised as an orphan, so she has no last name. She was chosen as the saint because she is the same age as Julius and has a straightforward and earnest personality. As a candidate for sainthood, she was above average but not exceptional, very talented for her age but not enough that she particularly stood out. As a result, though she does her best to be worthy of the title of saint, she feels a great deal of pressure. She sympathizes with Julius, since he is also under pressure because of his role as the hero and a prince. Her feelings toward him were already akin to love from the moment they met, but it didn't take long for her to completely fall head over heels for him.

Sophia's Diary 3

We had our school entrance ceremony.

That's it.

What?

You want to hear more?

Sure, we had to introduce ourselves to the other kids in our class afterward and all that, but why would I remember the names and faces of those nobodies?

Well, I suppose there were a *few* people who stood out to me.

Like the Goody Two-shoes boy who's definitely a jerk deep down.

And the idiotically serious class rep–type girl.

And a couple of snot-nosed brats who I *guess* might grow up to be beauties someday.

Basically, nobody who was worth my time.

Huh?

You think I can't make any friends?

That's none of your business! As if I want to do that anyway!

J4　JULIUS, AGE 12: SHOWDOWN

"It seems the enemy base is in a deserted village some distance from the mountain road."

Mr. Tiva spreads out a map as he explains.

Myself and the other commanding officers of the force listen in silence.

After our forces were caught in an ambush laid by the organization last time, a sudden sense of anxiety has taken hold.

Until then, things had been going almost alarmingly well.

So although the surprise attack hardly resulted in any casualties, the commanders seem to be trying to refocus their efforts after the force encountered its first stumbling block.

"The only route to the village is along this old road. Thus, the enemy will likely be on high alert for our approach."

All of us stare down at the map on the desk.

"This'll be tough," one commander murmurs.

The surprise-attack incident isn't the only reason the commanders look tense.

Our next target is a particularly difficult one.

The organization's presence here in this abandoned village is operating on a far larger scale than anything we've faced so far.

A deserted village is definitely troublesome.

Even if people no longer live there, pieces of their lives still remain in the area.

In other words, it's a base that's already furnished with much of what people need to survive.

Houses in which to sleep, fields for self-sufficient farming, most likely a nearby source of water, and walls to keep out monsters.

They'll have all of that at their disposal.

And this means they'll have a fairly stable livelihood, which in turn means other outlaws will be drawn there as well.

That means the village supports a high population, and numbers mean power.

No matter how high your stats are, it's difficult to make up for a sheer difference in numbers.

The only exception is someone with stats so high that being outnumbered doesn't make a difference—like me, the hero.

Of course, the force is made up of exceptions like that, since it consists of elite fighters drawn from various nations.

I'm sure each one of them could manage two or three bandits alone.

But that's before you take the enemy's home-field advantage into account.

According to our investigations, the village they're using as a base is practically a fortress.

And as Tiva said, the map shows that the only way to attack them is from the front.

The terrain makes this area difficult to attack and easy to defend.

Between the numbers and their field advantage, they might be able to make up for the difference in stats.

"Could we split up the troops?"

"No. The only other routes run straight through the mountains. We'd only be able to move through those in extremely small groups."

"Besides, the entire village is protected by walls. Whether we try to climb over or break through, we'll be spotted right away. We might be able to mount a surprise attack, but it'd be too dangerous for a small group."

"Hrmmm. Then I suppose we have no choice but to attack head-on and besiege them."

It's extremely difficult to move around on a mountain with no roads.

You have to cut your way through thick brush just to get anywhere, and you might run into monsters that live in the area, too.

It'd be impossible with a large group.

A small group would have to endure an arduous mountain trek, and right after, they would have to battle the bandits.

It's only natural that such a plan would be rejected out of hand.

But that's what heroes are for.

"I'll launch the surprise attack."

"Sir Hero...it's too dangerous."

The commander who chides me makes no attempt to hide his exasperation.

I can tell he's thinking, *Were you even listening?* and I understand how he feels.

But I can't back down now.

If I keep staying on the sidelines and letting them protect me, nothing will ever change.

I'm sure the reason I couldn't do anything before is that my resolve wasn't strong enough.

I wasn't ready to fight people, to kill.

But I'm ready now.

I just have to put that resolve into action.

So that I can save as many victims as possible and prevent as many future kidnappings as I can.

"Very well."

I open my mouth to protest, then freeze when I realize what I just heard.

Which probably leaves me looking like my mouth is hanging open idiotically.

I really am shocked by what he said, so I guess that impression wouldn't be wrong.

But everyone else in the room looks equally surprised.

The person who agreed with my plan is none other than Mr. Tiva.

"But of course, we cannot let you do this entirely alone, Sir Hero. I will send a few of my men along with you. And I happen to know a talented adventurer, so I'll ask him to accompany you as well."

Tiva briskly continues setting out the plan.

"Would you be willing to take this route through the mountains and attack the enemy from the rear?"

"Um, sure."

It's happening so quickly that I end up giving a dazed-sounding answer.

But then one of the commanders recovers his senses and leaps out of his chair.

"Sir Tiva! What in the world are you thinking?!"

"Whatever do you mean?"

Mr. Tiva stares back calmly, looking as if he truly doesn't understand the problem.

"We can't have Sir Hero do something so dangerous! What do you think he is?!"

"Ah, is that all you meant?"

"Is that *all*?!"

Tiva chuckles as if he's heard a particularly funny joke.

Anyone can see that he's mocking the commander. I didn't think he was the sort of person to do something like that, so I'm at a loss for words, too.

"Sir Hero volunteered for the role of his own free will. And I made the judgment that he's fully capable of it, so I am planning accordingly. What is the issue here?"

"The whole plan is rife with issues! What if something happens to Sir Hero? Will you take full responsibility for that?!"

Ah, this is it.

One of the invisible chains that binds me.

To the commanders, I'm a ward whose life must be protected, not a comrade to whom they can entrust their lives.

Words like *responsibility* make that clear.

"Why on earth would you bring up a word like *responsibility*?"

"What? Sir Tiva, please be reasonable."

The commander's irritation is increasingly obvious.

"Sir Hero is fully responsible for his own actions, of course. He is the high commander, and he can go to the front lines if he so chooses."

At that, the commander's mouth clamps shut.

"In fact, you've been voicing complaints about the high commander's decisions all this time. Is it safe to assume that you doubt the strength of Sir Hero, who is our leader?"

"What?! No, but...I..."

Once Tiva reminds him of my position, the commander recoils and seemingly runs out of excuses.

He looks to the other commanders for help, but they awkwardly avoid meeting his eyes.

I'm sure most of them agree with him, but they don't want to defend someone who's currently speaking out against their high commander—me—and earning stern disapproval from the deputy high commander, Mr. Tiva, in the process.

"But still! If the worst was to happen and something befell Sir Hero, the world would be at a loss! I beg you to reconsider!"

Realizing that no one is coming to his aid, the commander steels himself and doubles down on his original statement.

Considering my position, his view isn't entirely wrong.

But Mr. Tiva cuts him down with a glare.

"So you not only doubt Sir Hero's strength, but you also reject my judgment that he is capable of the job?"

It's as if the commander is no longer permitted to even explain himself.

"You asked me a moment ago what I think Sir Hero is, so I shall ask you the same. What is it that *you* think of Sir Hero, hmm?"

The commander has no response to Mr. Tiva's hard tone.

"This is exactly why Sir Hero does not have faith we will watch his back. How could he, when none of you thinks of him as a comrade in arms? It's no wonder he doesn't trust us."

"Mr. Tiva, that's—"

"There's no need to try and smooth things over, Sir Hero. This is all because we're so cowardly."

I open my mouth to object to his harsh self-criticism, but Mr. Tiva stops me.

"Besides, how many among you would even be a match for Sir Hero? Not a one, as far as I can see. Frankly, even I might fall short. What right do men weaker than Sir Hero have to decide his actions for him, then?"

A few of the commanders grow visibly angry at that last comment, but in the face of Tiva's fiery rage, they can't utter a word.

"We haven't supported Sir Hero at all. In fact, we can't even catch up to him. And yet, we all look down on him as if we've been protecting him, just because we are adults and he is a child. Do you know what that's called where I come from? Misplaced kindness."

SLAM! Mr. Tiva brings his fist down hard on the desk.

"We should be fighting by Sir Hero's side, but instead, we lag behind him—no, in fact, we're dragging him down! It's no wonder that he's given up on us and keeps attempting to act on his own!"

What?!

I think I might be more surprised by Mr. Tiva's anger than anyone else.

That's not what I was trying to do...

But the meeting room falls silent, and I don't have the courage to speak out.

"If you are concerned for Sir Hero's safety, then show that you have the mettle to bring down the enemy stronghold without needing Sir Hero to launch a surprise attack. But if you cannot do that, you're all bark and no bite."

I can see fighting spirit beginning to burn bright in the commanders' eyes.

They all climbed up to their current positions through sheer strength.

Now it seems that their pride in that strength means they're unable to back down after being so thoroughly reprimanded.

"Very well. I shall prove to you that I am more than just talk. We'll finish things before Sir Hero can even launch his attack—you shall see."

The commander who spoke up before glares at Mr. Tiva with a gleam in his eyes.

I guess they've accepted my surprise-attack plan, then.

When I realize this, it suddenly occurs to me that all of this might have played out exactly as Mr. Tiva planned.

As a result of his words, I get to lead an assault like I wanted, and he's even lit a fire beneath the commanders.

On top of that, they've practically promised not to complain next time if they aren't able to bring down the organization base before I launch my surprise attack.

Since they all have so much pride and belief in their own strength, I doubt the commanders would go back on their word or try to make excuses if they fail.

I estimate roughly how long it'll take me to get to the back of the enemy base from the foot of the mountain and how long it might take the men to bring down the fort from the front.

...There's no way they'll be able to do that before I can attack, as far as I can tell.

I can see that a few of the commanders are holding back sighs, so maybe they realize that, too.

So this was all part of Mr. Tiva's plan?

I always thought of Mr. Tiva as a thoughtful, discerning adult, but it looks like I should add *determined* and *not to be taken lightly* to that description.

More than anything, I'm glad he's on my side.

"This way, I reckon. Watch yer step there."

I follow the man with the unusual speech patterns deeper into the mountain.

My guide's name is Mr. Hawkin.

Apparently, he's a former thief and currently the slave of an adventurer.

"......"

Mr. Hawkin's master, Mr. Jeskan, walks ahead of me in silence.

He's striding along through this treacherous terrain as easily as if he was taking a stroll in town.

Yet he still seems to be on high alert: Occasionally, his eyes will shoot off to one side, moments before a bird or other small animal passes by.

I could never detect the presence of such small creatures. His Presence Perception skill level must be incredibly high.

That's to be expected, though—Mr. Jeskan is a famous adventurer.

He's climbed all the way up to A rank on his own with his ability to skill-fully use all kinds of different weapons based on what the situation calls for.

From what I'm told, he's still young and is expected to reach S rank soon enough, too.

Considering that Mr. Tiva referred to him as a capable adventurer and hired him to work with me, I'm sure he's trustworthy as well as incredibly strong.

That must be why he's allowed to bring a suspicious-seeming guide like a former thief.

But apparently, not everyone has accepted that.

"Why must we follow behind the likes of a former thief anyway?"

Yaana grumbles quietly.

She has an incredibly strong sense of justice and hates anything improper or immoral.

From her point of view, I'm sure a robber is worthy of nothing but contempt.

She doesn't seem to be able to accept working with one, even if he is a *former* thief.

"Mr. Hawkin isn't the kinda thief you're thinking of, Yaana," Hyrince explains. "He's a gentleman thief—he only stole from corrupt nobles and merchants to spread the wealth among the poor and needy."

Hyrince insisted it was natural for him to join this battle, since he's my attendant.

I was told that he negotiated with Mr. Tiva and convinced Tiva to let him come along with me.

"Is that true?!"

"Isn't that right, Mr. Thief with a Thousand Knives?"

At that, Mr. Hawkin peers back at us with a sly grin.

"Aw, shucks. That's just an old nickname o' mine."

"Th-the famous Thief with a Thousand Knives?! That's you?!"

The Thief with a Thousand Knives is Mr. Hawkin's old alias. He was a rogue who made quick work of any enemy with his knife skills and never let a target escape with their belongings.

He pursued only those who engaged in fraud and wrongdoing and delivered his earnings to orphanages and the needy in the form of food.

Since the anonymous donations were food, not stolen goods or coin, the nobles and merchants who'd been robbed couldn't take their money back, so the poor and hungry were always grateful to the Thief with a Thousand Knives.

And the person who carried out these fairy tale–like feats is none other than Mr. Hawkin.

Legends of his exploits have been spread far and wide by minstrels, and now you can hear them in many different lands.

In other words, Yaana had no idea she was complaining about someone very famous.

She looks embarrassed, although also a little disappointed.

"You're not quite what I imagined…"

Though she mutters it almost to herself, it carries surprisingly well on the mountain air.

Yaana blushes and hastily covers her mouth, but since everyone here is trained for battle, we all have the Five Senses Enhancement skill.

Everyone heard her as soon as she said it, which means Mr. Hawkin must have heard her initial complaint as well.

Which is probably why Hyrince covered for her in the first place.

"Heh, I get that a lot. It's always real pretty-boy types who play me in the theaters and stuff, so I can't blame ya."

Mr. Hawkin doesn't seem particularly offended.

Since the stories of the Thief with a Thousand Knives have become famous through minstrels, there are also plays about him, with the lead role usually going to the star actor of the troupe.

As a result, most people imagine the famous thief as a handsome young man, but I have to admit that you couldn't quite describe Mr. Hawkin that way even if you were being charitable.

He is surprisingly young, but his features are exceedingly ordinary, to the point where he could very easily blend into a crowd.

Maybe that's why he was such a good thief in the first place.

"But why is the Thief with a Thousand Knives a slave?"

This time, Yaana directs her suspicious gaze at Mr. Jeskan, Mr. Hawkin's master.

"Well, it's a funny story, that. See, I got caught by that human-trafficking organization yer all after and damn near lost my head. But Mr. Jeskan here was kind enough to buy little ol' me."

"I happened to be investigating the organization on a request from the government, which is why I was in touch with them. There's a limit to how much you can accomplish solo, so I gave the pretext that I wanted a slave who could fight, and here we are."

From the rest of their explanation, Mr. Hawkin was independently trying to gather information on the human-trafficking organization, while Mr. Jeskan was doing the same for a formal government request. In the process, Hawkin was captured, and since Jeskan had said he wanted a battle-ready slave, he ended up buying him.

"I'm real grateful, y'know. You saved my life."

"Well, you can pay me back by working hard."

Despite their relationship as master and slave, I can tell that these two get along quite well.

As proof, the collar has been removed from Mr. Hawkin's neck.

The human-trafficking organization puts special collars around their captives, which render the victim incapable of disobeying their master's orders.

We don't understand how it works exactly.

The collars are probably processed in a special way and conferred with some kind of control skill, or so I'm told, but even the researchers from the Word of God couldn't figure out anything else.

In other words, the human-trafficking organization has someone on their payroll whose technology outpaces that of the Word of God's research team.

Why would a seedy criminal organization have such technology?

There are a lot of mysteries, but it doesn't change what I have to do.

"Heh-heh. They shouldn't've let me go after allowin' me to see their hideout. They're gonna regret bein' so careless, I betcha."

Mr. Hawkin smirks.

The reason he's leading the way is that he was being held captive in the same deserted village that we're trying to attack now.

He was investigating the mountain area when he was caught, too, so he's the perfect guide.

As a former thief, he's an expert in finding routes that normally aren't noticeable and can spot and dismantle any traps along the way without breaking a sweat.

"There it is."

Thanks to Mr. Hawkin's expert guidance, we soon find ourselves at our destination: overlooking the back of the deserted village.

Contrary to what the phrase *deserted village* would suggest, its defenses look very sturdy.

It's all made of wood, but the walls surrounding the village are still solid, with a gate and even a watchtower built at the front facing the old road.

Just as our information said, it really is like a minor fortress.

Busting in from the front looks like a back-breaking task.

Sure enough, it sounds like the main force is still trying to contend with the front defenses. I can hear the clangs and cries of battle from that direction.

It looks like the commanders won't be able to bring down the fort before I can launch my surprise attack after all.

As I prepare my magic, I can't help smiling dryly to myself. *I guess Mr. Tiva was right as always.*

"Listen up, Julius. If all you want to do is use magic, skills are plenty for that. But if you truly want to master magic, that isn't good enough. How do you normally create and unleash spells? Be aware of that, and ask yourself how you can do it stronger, faster, and more accurately."

I remember my master's words.

He is a little bit crazy, but his teachings were right on the mark. He showed me exactly what I needed to do to be strong.

Following his instructions now, I focus hard on the magic I'm about to unleash.

"As soon as I break down the wall with magic, please charge in and attack."

After issuing an order to the rest of the group, I start to weave my spell.

"Now!"

In time with my shout, I cast the Holy Magic spell Holy Light Sphere.

The ball of light crashes into the wooden wall at high speed, breaking it down with a roar.

In its wake, nothing is left but a carved-out space of ground, not exactly an ideal entrance for an attack. Maybe I should've held back a bit more.

I guess I still have a long way to go.

"Charge!"

""""RAAAAH!""""

I call out to cover up my mistake, and together we all dash toward the village.

The members of the human-trafficking organization, fighting to defend the front gate, turn around in a panic when we burst through the destroyed wall.

I guess they weren't expecting a surprise attack to come through the rear wall.

The wooden barrier was certainly sturdy enough to keep out the weak monsters that roam in this area and would've been difficult to break down for any ordinary soldiers.

But in the face of a truly strong opponent, a palisade is useless.

In the former Keren County town of Sariella, even the stone walls that protected the village were meaningless in the face of those white spiders.

If I'm going to face that kind of enemy in the future, or maybe something even stronger, I can't let a little wall like this slow me down!

The bandits whirl around and try to fend us off.

But at the same time as our attack, the main forces renew their assault on the front gate, throwing the enemy's battle formations into disarray.

Spying a perfect opportunity, I speed up and charge into the enemy lines.

The man in front of me, who was in the rear of the bandit forces, can't even ready his weapon in his panic.

I slash my sword at my defenseless opponent, then move on to cut down the next one without stopping to see the results.

With each swing of my sword, I feel it bite into flesh and let a spray of blood fill the air.

The enemy soldiers fall one after another, scarcely even putting up a fight.

"Aaaaah!"

One of the remaining men charges at me desperately.

He swings his club around in the air, preparing to bring it down on me with sheer momentum.

"Ah!"

Then Hyrince jumps between the man and me, blocks the club with the shield in his left hand, and pierces the man's neck with the sword in his right.

"Quit going so far ahead, dumbass!"

"This is nothing!" I protest. "I'll keep going as far as I can!"

"Watch out!"

Just then, an arrow comes flying toward me, only to be struck down by Mr. Jeskan's sickle and chain in the nick of time.

"Thank you!"

With a brief thanks, I keep moving to the next opponent.

Jeskan uses a throwing ax to deftly dispatch the enemy soldier who shot the arrow.

Behind me, the rest of the group engages in battle with the enemy, while Yaana supports them with magic.

Farther ahead, my attack seems to have created enough of a gap for the main force to finally break down the front gate, and now our allies come pouring through in earnest.

At this point, the enemy has no way to stop us.

Our victory is cemented within minutes.

"Dammit! You bastards!"

One of the surviving enemy soldiers we've captured spits at us.

"What were we s'posed to do?! I was deep in debt! This was the only way I could keep on livin'. I had no choice! Don't you get it?!"

He's only lightly wounded, so he was the first of the prisoners to wake up, and he immediately started cursing us.

Doesn't he know what's going to happen to him?

"Hey, you, kid! I've got a son right around yer age! I can't go dyin' on him here! Please?!"

The man tries to reason with me as I happen to pass nearby.

One of the soldiers walking with me silently reaches for his sword, but I gesture for him to back down.

"No matter what the reason, it's never right to bring misfortune on others to solve your own."

With that, I leave the man behind.

He keeps shouting after me, but I doubt I'll get through to him, no matter what I say.

People turn to the path of evil far too easily.

I've seen that while traveling with this special task force, far more than I ever wanted to.

The human-trafficking organization has all kinds of members.

Some turned to crime in order to put food on the table, like this man.

Others were forced to join the organization despite their young age because their parents were members.

And still others seemed evil by nature, simply taking pleasure in seeing others suffer.

Each of them had joined the human-trafficking organization under different circumstances.

But there was one thing they all had in common: None of them regretted it.

Not a single one seemed to regret having stained their hands with evil.

Of course, some of them claimed to be remorseful when it came time for execution.

But they weren't really repenting for their sins—they were just sorry they'd been caught and were being punished.

Why couldn't I have gotten away with it?

That's the awful truth of what they were thinking.

There were times when I tried to convince them to start anew with the right words.

But of course, I had to move on to the next battle.

People turn to evil easily.

And it takes untold time and patience to turn them back to the right path.

So fast to fall and so difficult to bring back to the light.

There are many different ways for a person to stray down the path of evil, but in order for them to return, they first need to regret the things they've done.

If you can't get them to realize how horrible their crimes were, then it's impossible to convince them to try to start over.

But I don't have that kind of time, and neither do they.

I have to travel to countless different lands, and they have to face a punishment that befits the weight of their crimes.

And in most cases, that means being tortured for information, then executed.

Even if we did have time to rehabilitate them, it'd be more effective to use the ones who can be used and dispose of the rest.

Because it's far more important to rescue the innocent victims still suffering at the hands of the human-trafficking organization than to dwell on these criminals.

I understand that, in theory.

But I don't know if I really believe that's right.

Some of them were participating only because they didn't have a choice.

They were poor, their hometowns were attacked by monsters, or they were born into it.

Is it really right to punish them without offering them a chance at rehabilitation?

...I might not be able to answer that, no matter how hard I agonize over it.

But still, I should always think about what I consider right and wrong, like Mr. Tiva said.

It's just that at the moment, there's only so much I can do.

My time is better spent rescuing many innocent victims from suffering than laboring to convince one person to turn their life around.

It's impossible to measure the value of a person's life, but between someone who's gravely sinned and someone who hasn't, it should be obvious which one should take priority.

Maybe things would be different if I had some other way to persuade those who have gone astray.

But I do not, so I have to prioritize saving the people who I can still save.

In a perfect world, I would save everyone, but I know that's not really possible.

I just have to do my absolute best to save as many people as I can.

No matter how difficult that might be.

Because that's what a hero does.

Special Chapter   THE FORMER THIEF AND THE ADVENTURER

"Are you worried about him?"

Hawkin's gaze is focused on the hero.

"Hey, boss. Yeah, I guess a little…"

Hawkin nods absently at my question.

Clearly, he's more than a little worried.

Hawkin loves children, so much so that it's the very reason he became a thief: to help as many children as possible avoid unhappy fates.

For someone so deeply immersed in the dark underbelly of society, he can be quite naive.

Although I must admit that I don't hate that about him.

"What d'you think, boss?"

I hesitate for a moment about how to answer Hawkin's vague question.

But then I decide to answer with my honest thoughts.

"He's very impressive, for sure."

At his young age, the hero already surpasses most adults.

Not just in combat but in spirit, too.

The way he stayed so calm while leading an attack on the organization base and fighting those bandits is proof enough of that.

Even an adult would normally be reluctant to cut down another person if they're not used to doing it, but he didn't show any hint of hesitation.

How many battles has he already fought, to reach that level at such a young age?

Not to mention, he's strong enough to lay waste to a wide swathe of the enemy base all on his own.

I jumped in to protect him at one point, but I suspect he would've been able to dodge that arrow whether or not he had my help.

He even had the composure to thank me.

And yet...

"But I guess that's exactly what has you worried, hmm?"

If he's that advanced at his age, that means he must have been through quite a lot.

And no matter how mature he might seem as a result, he is still a child.

If you put a child through such awful experiences one after another, he might eventually break down.

I'm sure that's what Hawkin is concerned about.

"Well, there's no need for you to worry about that. As far as I can tell, Sir Tiva is keeping a close eye on the situation. With his title as the Hero, I doubt Julius will ever have a normal childhood, but it shouldn't be too horrible, either."

My interaction with the deputy high commander Sir Tiva was brief, but I got a very strong impression of him. The boy is his superior officer, but he respects him as a hero while also caring for him as a human being.

As long as that man is by the hero's side, I'm sure he won't let anything unthinkable happen to him.

I can't help but notice that my reassurances fail to clear up the shadow hanging over Hawkin's face, though.

"Why does a kid like that have to fight, y'know?"

Hawkin is a permanent citizen of the underworld, and I'm sure he knows it as well as I do.

But he still resents the injustices of this world, enough so that he can't help saying things like that.

This man really is naive.

But I think the world needs people like him, too.

Especially when it comes to the symbol of goodness called the hero.

"I asked Sir Tiva to let us officially join the force."

At that, Hawkin looks up with a gasp.

"If you're that worried, we can just protect him from close by. I was starting to feel like I'd reached my limit as a solo adventurer anyway. Helping the hero is a prestigious role, so it all works out great. Right?"

"Boss...thank you."

There's nothing to thank me for, so I simply respond with a shrug.

And that's how Hawkin and I join the task force.

Sophia's Diary 4

Ugh, I'm so mad!

Why am I so mad, you ask?

That Goody Two-shoes keeps coming after me, that's why!

All while making it look like he's not doing it at all!

He'll talk to me in this suuuper-nice-sounding voice, saying things like, *Oh yeah, I can do this and that. What about you?*

And when I respond that I can do it, he praises me for it.

But his eyes are laughing at me!

He'll ask the other kids in class the same thing, and if they say they can't, he'll be all, *Let me know if I can help; I'd be happy to teach you!*

The other boys and girls all fall for it right away, but I know this is just his way of asserting dominance.

He wants to make sure he's at the top of the pecking order.

Huh?

You think I'm being paranoid?

Tsk, tsk, tsk.

You're so naive.

Listen up, okay?

The hierarchy of a class is extremely important!

Your school life changes VERY dramatically based on where you stand in the rankings!

The top tier has it made—the picture-perfect school life.

The middle isn't great but not awful, either. You could definitely still have a decent time in your youth.

But the bottom rung? Forget it.

You'll either be driven into a corner and forced to scurry around every day like you don't even exist, or you'll be subjected to the brunt of the bullying!

...I seem to know a lot about this, you say?

Well, yeah. I was in the bottom tier in my previous life.

Hey, don't feel sorry for me!

Stop! Don't look at me like that, okay?!

J5   Julius, Age 13: Machinations

I walk through the familiar halls of the Analeit Kingdom castle.

In other words, my childhood home.

Since becoming the hero, I've been primarily staying in the room given to me in the Holy Kingdom of Alleius, so I haven't been here in a while, but I still think of it as my real home.

Being in this place calms me in a way that the room in Alleius never could. But that's just me.

Clinging to my arm as we walk, Yaana looks incredibly nervous.

Instead of her usual saint outfit, which is simple and designed for easy movement, she's wearing a white dress.

It's an understated design, as befits a saint, but you can still see at a glance how expensive it must be.

It was made specifically for Yaana, so it looks great on her.

…Or at least, it would if her face wasn't currently so strained that her tension is plainly obvious.

Her movements are equally stiff, to the point where I'm not sure if she'd be able to walk without falling over if I wasn't escorting her.

Yaana and I have come here to participate in a certain ceremony.

This is Yaana's first time in the royal castle, and she was incredibly anxious on the way here about what it would be like.

As with many girls her age, she seemed to have a certain admiration for the romantic idea of a castle.

She didn't say that in so many words, but Yaana is always easy to read, so I could tell she was excited.

But now that we're actually here, her nerves seem to have overtaken any other emotions.

Knowing her serious personality, she's probably putting an absurd amount of pressure on herself, thinking that she can't do anything to embarrass herself as the saint.

"Yaana."

At this rate, I feel as though she's actually even more likely to embarrass herself, so I stop her before we enter the ceremonial hall.

She turns around with an almost audible creak, like a door whose hinges badly need to be oiled.

"Are you nervous?"

"Of…course…not."

That's not very convincing when her voice is so hesitant, and so quiet I can barely hear it.

"You are, aren't you?"

"…Yes, I am. I'm sorry."

She looks pained, but I think her inability to lie is one of her virtues.

Although she probably wouldn't survive for long in high society.

"It's perfectly normal to be nervous," I assure her.

Yaana may be the saint, but she's not from a noble family, so she hasn't participated in many formal ceremonies like this one.

She might have worked on them behind the scenes while she was training as a sainthood candidate, but I'm guessing the only time she's actually been a part of one is when she was actually appointed as the saint, so she's still inexperienced.

"I know I mustn't be nervous, but I can't help it…" Her voice trembles.

"No, I don't think there's anything wrong with that."

She seems to feel that it's wrong to be nervous, but I assure her that the opposite is true.

Yaana blinks at me uncertainly, as if she doesn't understand.

"If you think you shouldn't be nervous, you'll just make it even worse. But it's normal to be nervous at times like these, so you're better off not trying to force yourself to be calm."

"But…"

"There's a level of nervousness that's just right. Do you know what I mean?"

During battle and such, it's better to be a little bit on edge than to be completely at ease.

Of course, if you're too nervous, you won't be able to function, like Yaana right now.

But nerves aren't necessarily a bad thing, even if it's hard to moderate them in the moment.

If you can keep it at the right level, it helps you focus and stay on your toes.

"I don't mind being nervous. And there's no need to be overly focused on not failing. If you do your best in the moment, I think good results will naturally follow. So try to let a little bit of the tension out of your shoulders, okay? It'd be a waste if you're too nervous to be your best self."

Yaana nods slowly, as if she's absorbing what I said.

"You're amazing, Sir Julius. Your words truly resonate, unlike a certain someone's."

I'm sure she's referring to Hyrince.

He must have been teasing her again, as usual.

"Just remember, that certain someone will be in the hall, too."

If she stays nervous and stiff throughout the ceremony, I'm sure Hyrince will tease her about it later. As I hint at this gently, Yaana's eyes widen.

I can't let that happen! is written all over her face.

Her eyes fill with newfound determination to avoid being teased.

They say that fighting proves the closeness of a friendship, but I'm not sure if that applies to Yaana and Hyrince.

It's more like Hyrince is toying with Yaana or holding her in the palm of his hand.

At any rate, it looks like that calmed her nerves a little, so hopefully now she won't make any major mistakes.

As long as she doesn't get too jittery and end up going overboard instead.

"Shall we go in, then?"

"Yes!"

We walk toward the ceremonial hall with lighter steps than before.

Soon, we reach the grand doors and walk inside, where there's already a big crowd.

The ceremony hasn't started yet, but the room is quiet, even though there are people gathered in the center.

Yaana seems unnerved by the strange atmosphere, but I tug her arm lightly and reassure her with a smile.

We walk deeper into the hall, reaching the far end where the royal family stands.

Everyone else is already there: the true queen; my elder brother, Cylis; the king's first and second concubines; and my younger brother Leston.

"You're late," Cylis informs me, looking displeased.

He never used to be like this, but lately, he always seems to be wearing an irritated scowl.

"I'm very sorry. I was so nervous over my little brother and sister having their big day that I scarcely slept last night, so I'm afraid I'm still a bit tired."

Yaana shoots me a doubtful glance at my excuse.

Obviously, I'm not really tired. We were late only because I was calming Yaana's nerves.

I lied because I didn't want to tell anyone else that, but Yaana's reaction probably made that a wasted effort.

Since my royal relatives spend their days studying their fellow courtiers for even the subtlest hints of thought or emotion, I imagine they all will have guessed from this exchange that I was covering for Yaana.

"Now, now, dear brother. It's not as though they've missed the start of the ceremony, so there's no need to glare at them so, is there?"

Leston intervenes with our elder brother on my behalf, but it only has the opposite effect.

"Worry about yourself, Leston. You ought to be calling me Elder Brother during a ceremony like this, not addressing me so casually."

Cylis's rage turns on Leston instead, although it's possible that Leston did that deliberately to draw his attention away from Yaana and me.

Leston might seem easygoing, but he can actually be fairly shrewd.

"That's quite enough."

As the argument between my brothers threatens to escalate, a cold, brisk voice interrupts them: the true queen.

"But, Mother..."

"Look around you. Do not bring any further shame on the royal family with your unseemly behavior."

Her biological son, Cylis, flinches at her scolding.

Realizing that the crowd is watching our interactions, he smooths over his expression.

"Please pardon my son's lapse in manners."

The queen apologizes to Yaana, but she doesn't bow her head.

Nor does she deign to introduce herself.

In the Analeit Kingdom, it's considered proper for the person of lower social status to introduce themselves first.

Yaana is the saint and comes from the Holy Kingdom of Alleius, so she doesn't have any particular hierarchical relationship with the queen.

But she's participating in this ceremony as my partner.

I am the hero, but in the Analeit Kingdom, I rank below the queen.

If the queen introduces herself first, then she'll indirectly be implying to everyone around us that she is below me in social standing; if Yaana goes first, it might seem as if she's debasing the Holy Kingdom of Alleius.

It's difficult to say whether Yaana should introduce herself first.

"Allow me to introduce my companion. This is Lady Yaana the saint, who is here today as my partner."

The best move is probably for me to introduce her instead.

Yaana must still be nervous; she gives a stiff curtsy without saying a word.

I'm not sure if that was her best option, but in the strange power dynamic this situation has created, it's not the worst one, either.

"Thank you for looking after our Julius."

The queen stares at Yaana appraisingly as she responds.

"N-not at all. If anything…Sir Julius is always…l-looking after me…"

…She's completely tongue-tied.

I guess the nerves I tried to dispel must have come back in full force.

Still, I can't say I blame her.

Anyone would wither under the true queen's cold glare if they're not accustomed to it. She's a very intimidating person.

"The ceremony will begin shortly. I'm afraid it may be quite dull in the interim, but please wait patiently."

The queen seems to have lost interest in Yaana, and she faces forward again.

My brothers and the concubines follow her lead, closing their mouths and standing at attention.

Yaana looks like she could burst into tears at any minute, so I whisper "it's okay" to her and line up next to the rest of the royal family.

Although, truth be told, I'm not sure if it's really okay or not...

I think the queen may have passed judgment on Yaana in that brief interaction and deemed her a person of no particular importance, someone she can ignore.

The fact that Yaana never got a chance to introduce herself is proof enough of that.

The true queen's steely gaze is difficult to read, so to be honest, I rarely know what she's thinking.

My father has two faces, that of a politician and that of a parent, but the queen only ever seems to show the former.

She's a model politician, in a different way from the pontiff.

The pontiff is always working on several schemes behind his gentle smile, but the queen simply masks everything with a cold glare.

That's always been my experience, at least.

So I don't know exactly what she really thought of Yaana.

But no matter what she might think deep down, I'm sure her attitude will never change.

As long as Yaana is the saint, she should at least have a modicum of respect for that position.

I'm just not sure if the same thing applies to Yaana herself.

"His Majesty has arrived."

After several more minutes of that same strange tension, the ceremony finally begins.

My father enters the room and stands behind a pedestal near the back.

"Prince Schlain and Princess Suresia have arrived."

Next, the names of my youngest siblings are announced.

A door opens opposite the pedestal, and Schlain and Sue enter.

They walk slowly and deliberately along the red carpet in the center of the room.

You could even describe their strides as dignified, despite their young age.

They don't seem nervous at all; they carry themselves with pride, as if it's only natural that everyone in the room is looking at them, and murmurs of admiration ripple through the crowd.

Finally, Schlain and Sue reach the pedestal and kneel.

"The Appraisal ceremony will now begin," our father announces.

Today is Schlain and Sue's Appraisal ceremony.

I took a leave of absence from the task force to be here for it.

The rest of the unit is still working without us, which pains me a little, but Mr. Tiva kindly encouraged me to bear witness to my young siblings' day in the spotlight.

Since we defeated the branch of the human-trafficking organization that had settled in the deserted village, the commanders have stopped complaining about my actions, in keeping with their promise to Mr. Tiva.

Thus, I've been able to take a more prominent role on the front lines, while Mr. Tiva gives orders from the rear.

Knowing that Tiva is supporting me from behind, I can focus on fighting without reserve.

And he's continued to help me along the way, admonishing the commanders when necessary.

As a result, the commanders are slowly starting to acknowledge me, all thanks to Mr. Tiva's efforts.

I can't thank him enough for all that he's done for me.

"Now, Schlain Zagan Analeit. You may rise."

"Yes, sir."

I wasn't sure whether I should participate in this ceremony, but now I'm glad I came.

My younger brother Schlain was already mature for his age, but he's grown even more than I expected.

I wish our mother could've watched him grow up as well, but I'll just have to pay even closer attention for her sake.

But my emotional moment quickly passes.

When Schlain's Appraisal results magically project onto the wall, the silence in the ceremonial hall shatters.

<Human   LV 1   Name   Schlain Zagan Analeit

Status: HP: 35/35 (green)   MP: 348/348 (blue)

             SP: 35/35 (yellow)   : 35/35 (red)

             Average Offensive Ability: 20 (details)   Average Defensive Ability: 20 (details)

             Average Magical Ability: 314 (details)   Average Resistance Ability: 299 (details)

             Average Speed Ability: 20 (details)

Skills: Skill Points: 100,000   Titles: None

[Magic Perception LV 8]	[Magic Operation LV 8]	[Magic Warfare LV 6]	[Magic Conferment LV 5]
[Magic Attack LV 3]	[MP Recovery Speed LV 7]	[MP Lessened Consumption LV 2]	[Swordsmanship LV 3]
[Destruction Enhancement LV 2]	[Mental Warfare LV 2]	[Energy Conferment LV 1]	[Concentration LV 5]
[Hit LV 1]	[Evasion LV 1]	[Vision Enhancement LV 4]	[Auditory Enhancement LV 7]
[Olfactory Enhancement LV 2]	[Taste Enhancement LV 1]	[Tactile Enhancement LV 1]	[Life LV 5]
[Magic Mass LV 8]	[Instantaneous LV 5]	[Persistent LV 5]	[Strength LV 5]
[Solidity LV 5]	[Technique User LV 8]	[Protection LV 7]	[Running LV 5]
[Divine Protection]	[n% I = W]		

>

His stats and skills are leagues beyond any normal child participating in their first Appraisal ceremony.

That's all well and good; Schlain has always been exceptional.

Even without my personal bias, he's objectively a child prodigy.

I'm not too surprised by his stats.

But the Divine Protection skill…that's far more alarming.

It's practically a declaration that Schlain is a special person, loved and favored by the gods.

I glance sideways at the true queen.

But her expression is as rigid as ever, revealing nothing of her thoughts.

After the ceremony, we move on to the next phase: a celebratory party.

But unfortunately, my feelings are too conflicted to properly celebrate.

"Yo. Should the great hero really be hiding out in a corner over here?"

Hyrince quickly spots Yaana and me taking refuge against the wall.

"Schlain and Sue are the stars today, so I figured it's better if we don't stand out too much."

"I guess." Hyrince shrugs.

Normally, Yaana would have some choice words for Hyrince's casual attitude, but today she's quiet as a mouse.

Hyrince, in turn, refrains from teasing her like he usually would.

He's capable of being considerate when it's really important, although I wish he'd do it all the time.

"What about you, Hyrince? Shouldn't you be congratulating Schlain and Sue, too?"

Hyrince is actually the second son of Duke Quarto, though it's easy to forget that at times.

As a member of a high-ranking noble family that's close to the royal family, he should really pay his respects to the stars of the day.

"Well, I figured, since I'm connected to you, I'll have a chance to talk to them soon enough. For now, I'd rather not stand around in that line."

Hyrince nods toward the long line in the center of the ballroom with a dry smile, where people are waiting for the chance to greet my siblings.

Only the highest-ranking nobles were allowed to attend the Appraisal ceremony, but this after-party includes a certain amount of lesser nobles as well.

Specifically, the ones who have children close in age to Schlain and Sue.

So now, the nobles are lining up in the hopes of getting their children close to the pair and potentially forming a connection to the royal family.

Although, considering the results of the Appraisal ceremony, I'm worried that there might be more to their motivations than just that.

"This is going to be a problem," Hyrince observes.

"…Yeah."

"What?"

Yaana looks between us in confusion.

Instead of explaining, I offer her the cake I grabbed from one of the waiters, since I'd noticed her glancing at it repeatedly.

Immediately, her eyes sparkle.

Oh, Yaana. Never change.

"So what should we do?"

"Nothing. Unfortunately, there's not really anything we *can* do."

Since I'm working with the special task force, there's not much I can do about the internal affairs of my kingdom.

Even my influence as the hero doesn't have much effect here.

The true queen's influence is too strong.

She has most of the nobles under her thumb, too.

And as far as this current incident goes, I have to be even more cautious of those who aren't affiliated with her.

"I guess we just have to hope that His Majesty and the queen will keep the idiots in check."

"Yeah."

Yaana still seems intrigued by our exchange, but she can't resist taking a bite of the cake.

Though she doesn't seem to understand, Hyrince and I are concerned that there might be movements to position Schlain as the next king.

Power struggles exist to some extent in most any nation, I think.

The Analeit Kingdom is no exception, with nobles conspiring behind the scenes day in and day out.

And in the past few years, there have been whispers of whether Prince Cylis is truly suited for the throne.

Cylis is the true queen's only son, and while I would never say this aloud, he's fairly ordinary.

His grades, combat skills, and everything else about him are all average.

My elder brother is making every effort to be worthy of inheriting the throne. It's just not yielding the results he wants.

But he's not below average in any way, either.

With the proper support, he'd make a perfectly acceptable king.

So the fact that Cylis is the only heir has never been a problem.

But frankly, my existence has complicated things.

I'm the hero—the only person in the world to receive this special title.

And I'm a prince of this kingdom, too.

However, that doesn't mean I'm in the running to be the next king.

The hero has never been the leader of a kingdom.

In fact, considering the hero's role, I don't think that would be possible—because the hero has to constantly fight against demons.

The only possible exception I can think of is the sword-king of the Renxandt Empire, which is humanity's bulwark that sits on the border we share with the demon realm.

The sword-king's job might overlap with that of the hero enough for it to work.

But aside from that exception, though there have been heroes born to royal families in the past, they've never become king. And I have no intention of trying to do so, either.

But what if the hero had an exceptional younger brother?

A prince who's related to the hero already has considerable appeal.

But if he also happens to be remarkably talented, and even boasts a skill called Divine Protection?

And currently, the true queen and her entourage stands at the heart of this kingdom.

Nobles who aren't associated with her party would likely jump at any chance to bring down the queen's son, my older brother, Cylis, and put someone else in power who'd be more favorable toward them.

Since I'm the hero, it's difficult for me to stay in the kingdom.

And the third son, my younger brother Leston, has been distancing himself from the nobles to avoid that kind of power struggle, deliberately making himself into a sort of prodigal son.

So it's only natural that the nobles would set their sights on the remaining son, Schlain.

With all these factors in place, they're certain to make their move.

"Fortunately, the situation is relatively stable right now. Unless they're incredibly stupid, nobody would make a move to try and depose Prince Cylis and put Prince Schlain in line for the throne right now."

"I hope you're right."

It's not just minor nobles who are resistant to the true queen's party right now.

Some of them are important figures, who could very well cause unexpected chaos.

Even thinking about it causes a sense of unease to rise up from my feet—especially when it's Schlain who could be at the center of it all.

"Whoa, wait a sec. Your brother's pretty on the ball, huh? He's already running off with a girl at his age!"

"What?"

I turn around in a hurry, just in time to see Schlain taking a girl by the hand and running out of the room.

"Who is that?"

"That's Duke Anabald's daughter, I think. I want to say her name is Karnatia? Your little bro's got a good eye."

"She certainly was cute."

"What?! Is that the kind of girl you like, Sir Julius?!"

Holding the plate of cake in one hand, Yaana suddenly chimes in to the conversation in a high-pitched voice.

"No, of course not. I wouldn't look at such a young girl that way."

"R-right..."

After my speedy denial, Yaana looks somehow relieved and returns to eating her cake.

...She seems to be especially conscious of me lately.

This could be bad.

"Duke Anabald is more moderate than the true queen's party. He doesn't get too close to her, but he doesn't stay too far away, either, putting him in an unusual position. So neither side can really lay a hand on him easily. Schlain's pretty sharp—he must have invited that girl for exactly that reason."

"I'm sure that's just a coincidence. How would Schlain know about those kinds of relationships and power struggles at his age?"

Although in Schlain's case, I can't entirely rule it out.

My younger brother sometimes speaks of strange proverbs or fairy tales that even I've never heard of; I've overheard him telling Sue strange stories, like "Momotarou" and "Issun-Boushi."

Where in the world did he get such knowledge?

At first I suspected his maid, Anna, but she doesn't seem to be the source.

Since I still don't know where he learned these things, I can't rule out that he might have deliberately chosen Duke Anabald's daughter.

Even when I asked him, he just told me that it comes from his dreams.

...Did he really dream all those things?

What if that's actually an effect of his mysterious Divine Protection skill? If that skill could cause divine revelations of a sort, it would explain a lot.

But whether he approached Anabald's daughter by coincidence or divine intervention, I guess it wouldn't change the situation at hand.

"Either way, Schlain's too young for all that."

"That's how royal engagements tend to go, though."

"Engagements?!"

A few heads turn toward us at Yaana's loud screech.

She gasps and covers her mouth, but it's too late.

Yaana looks to me for help, but all I can do is smile weakly.

Even Hyrince is wincing, and for once, it doesn't seem to be an act.

"...Well, now what? Rumors tend to get blown out of proportion fast. I bet everyone will be saying that Prince Schlain and Lady Karnatia are engaged by tomorrow."

"I don't think there's much we can do, especially when they were holding hands like close friends. It's probably too late."

"Huh? What?! Did I do something wrong?!"

"It's fine."

I hand Yaana a second plate of cake to calm her down.

Her gaze goes back and forth between my face and the cake but finally settles on the latter.

The moment Schlain and Miss Karnatia did such a conspicuous thing, it was probably inevitable that they'd be the subject of rumors.

Admittedly, Yaana probably added fuel to the fire by shouting about an engagement, but I don't think what she did was all that bad.

Besides, like Hyrince said, it's not necessarily bad for Schlain to be linked to Duke Anabald's family.

If anything, an engagement to Karnatia would probably be a good thing for him—if you didn't take his feelings into account or one other major problem.

If Schlain really did fall for Karnatia at first sight or something like that, then I'd be happy to cheer them on.

But there's one other serious issue.

"Uh-oh. Suresia is ignoring His Majesty's orders and chasing after them."

"Yeah, looks that way."

I chuckle dryly as I gaze at the biggest obstacle to Schlain's potential engagement: his half sister, Sue, flying into a rage as I expected.

"Uh, I just heard a pretty serious crash. Think they're okay?"

"...Maybe not."

A loud noise echoes through the room, audible even over the considerable chatter.

I'm sure everyone can hear it.

The knights in charge of guarding the hall hurriedly jump into action, and it looks like they might even start evacuating people.

Since I have an inkling of what might be going on, I can't help but groan.

"Sorry, Hyrince, but do you mind telling the guards there's no need to cause a commotion?"

"Got it."

At times like this, it's great to have a friend who'll do what you ask without any further explanation.

Yaana is flailing nervously, holding her second empty plate.

"I'm sorry, Yaana. Can you wait here quietly for a minute?"

Considering the disaster I might need to rein in, it'd be difficult to look after her on top of everything else.

I feel bad leaving her here alone, but she'll have to manage.

With that, I half walk, half sprint toward the source of the sound.

Then there's a second crash.

Cold sweat runs down my back as I quicken my pace.

When I arrive at the small room, I see pretty much exactly what I feared: a broken door, a pale Miss Karnatia, and Sue clinging tightly to Schlain.

Schlain's one massive problem is that his half sister, Sue, is completely in love with him.

Half siblings or not, it's bad enough for a blood relative to have romantic feelings for him, but the intensity of Sue's attachment makes it far worse.

According to Schlain, girls who express their love like Sue does are called *yandere*, whatever that means.

If Schlain gets engaged, Sue is liable to seriously hurt the girl in question.

Fortunately, it doesn't look like she's done anything to Karnatia this time, but she's definitely shooting her a murderous glare.

"Are you hurt?"

"I-I'm fine."

First, I make sure that Karnatia is safe.

"Sue, you know you shouldn't do things like that."

"It's that harlot's fault for trying to seduce my brother!"

"Oh, Sue..."

I try to scold her, but she doesn't seem remotely sorry.

"At any rate, you've got to let go of Schlain. Can't you see he's having trouble breathing?"

As Sue wraps her arms around him tightly, a faint groan escapes Schlain's lips.

"My dear brother can surely handle my love."

"I'm not so sure about that, so please let him go."

Sue refuses to listen, so I forcibly peel her away from Schlain.

"Thank you." He coughs.

"Schlain, you should also be careful about indulging Sue too much, okay? If you want her to stop, say so."

"My dear brother would never reject me."

"Oof...you're right. I'll deal with it."

Schlain winces, while Sue seems to be bragging for some reason.

I heave a sigh at the whole situation.

Meanwhile, Karnatia looks on, dumbfounded, throughout the whole exchange.

I can't say I blame her.

It's extra clear now that Schlain's going to have some serious struggles with women from here on out.

Just as I'm about to let the knights know things have calmed down, the king and queen appear outside the room.

My father looks worried, while the true queen is expressionless as always.

What is she thinking as she looks at Schlain?

Romance isn't the only thing that Schlain might have some problems with; there are a lot of difficulties likely waiting for him down the road.

I walk toward the king and queen.

"Everything's fine now."

"Oh? I'm glad to hear it."

My father presses a hand to his chest in relief.

"Could you look after Schlain, please?"

"Of course."

When I make a request to my father with deeper meaning behind the words, he agrees right away.

The queen, however, says nothing.

As his older brother, I'll have to do whatever I can to ensure that he has a happy future.

"…What did you just say?"

The day after Schlain and Sue's Appraisal ceremony, I receive some seemingly impossible news.

"Sir Tiva has fallen in battle."

The day after celebrating my younger siblings' triumph, I lose someone incredibly dear to me.

Special Chapter — THE EMPIRE VETERAN'S FINAL HOURS

I decided to join the anti-human-trafficking task force out of a personal grudge.

My son and his wife finally had a child, and the sword-king's first child was born around the same time, so the entire empire seemed to be in a celebratory mood.

In retrospect, I'm sure that I must have been, too.

Perhaps that is why I didn't stop my son and his family from going out without a security detail, a decision I regret to this day.

I never would have let my guard down like that during the war with the demons.

"Guards? There's no need for that. Do you think your own son so weak that I can't even protect myself?"

Why didn't I push back against my son's confident words?

In fact, I even remember being impressed with him.

If only I had warned him then that such pride would be the death of him, perhaps the future would have been different.

My son and his family never returned and were found dead the next day.

A carriage accident...or so it was made to look like.

In reality, my son, his wife, and their child were all assassinated by an unknown culprit.

I searched for the perpetrator like a man possessed, using any means available to me to gather every last clue connected to the crime.

My son was not weak, just as he proudly pointed out to me.

Since he was born after the demons quieted down, he didn't have much battle experience, but he was still my pride and joy.

He was strong, enough to be a match for most men, save for experienced old souls like me.

Among his peers, youths who never experienced war, he was certainly one of the strongest.

But someone killed my son with incredibly practiced ease.

Given the methods and strength that must have taken, no doubt there was a bigger scheme at work.

And at the same time, the disappearances that were likely kidnappings began.

It didn't take long to connect the two, nor to determine that there was a large organization behind them.

My only miscalculation was the sheer size of that organization.

I never imagined the same kidnappings were taking place all over the world, not just in the empire. While I knew it was large, I'd assumed it was limited to this area, but it far surpassed my expectations.

If the organization was only in the empire, I could have chased them down myself.

But now that the search had to expand to other countries, it was too much for even me to handle on my own.

Perhaps it would have been feasible were it only the empire and our neighboring allies, but the scope of the organization transcended even the continent, in places where the empire would hold no authority.

Even in the lands of our allies, it would be difficult to investigate without the proper justification, and a great deal of preparation and paperwork would be involved.

By the time I was nearly done crushing the organization within the empire, there was already little else I could do.

But then I received the news.

The Holy Kingdom of Alleius was forming a special task force that would transcend all borders, in order to hunt down the human-trafficking organization on a massive scale.

And since I was already fighting the organization within our empire, I was invited to participate.

Of course, I agreed without a moment's hesitation.

If I joined the force, I could legally investigate and weed out the organization's branches in other lands.

I had no doubt that the Holy Kingdom of Alleius had its own motivations for creating the force, having recently failed to take over Sariella, but that mattered little to me.

My motivations for joining the force were not anything noble, like protecting other families from becoming victims. I joined with the sole intention of avenging my son and his family.

Of course, I was also determined to save the children who were kidnapped in the empire, especially Buirimus's daughter.

But my deep-seated grudge was the greatest deciding factor.

I would destroy the organization and take revenge for my son, his wife, and my grandchild.

I do acknowledge I did the great sword-king wrong by leaving.

Temporary or not, my absence left a considerable hole in the empire. For whatever reason, I hold strong influence over the military there.

The sword-king already has many enemies, so my absence likely put him in a precarious situation.

He probably placed me in charge of raising his son for that very reason, in the hopes of keeping me in the empire, but my reasons for hunting the organization were simply too strong.

Thus, I joined the special task force to hunt down the traffickers.

I was given the role of deputy to the high commander: the second-in-command over the entire force.

But since the actual commander was the young hero, I essentially stood at the top.

I used this position to devote myself to rooting out the organization.

Investigating every nation, determining which bases were the most important and which would be the most effective to attack.

I made all these decisions and successfully guided the force.

The force is a mishmash of soldiers from many different regions.

Individually, they're all elite fighters, but it's difficult to rein them all in under a clear chain of command.

Whenever we discussed our next course of action, each of the commanders would insist on their own wishes, making progress difficult.

But I managed to push through and used my position as deputy high commander to have the final word on these long debates and move things forward.

I wonder how many of them noticed that I was really just forcing my own intentions on them.

But I know that I was choosing the strategies that would be most effective for crushing the human-trafficking organization, which is the goal of the force, so I doubt anyone would complain even if they did realize it.

Though I felt for the hero, who was forced to be purely a figurehead in his role as high commander, I intended to let it be a life lesson to him and continue on this way.

Sir Hero is still so young.

I thought that if he experienced this kind of dissatisfactory situation early on, he would be better equipped to deal with it later in life.

The role of hero comes with many adult obligations.

So he ought to get used to such restraints and learn when to abide by them, when to shake them off, and when to use them to his own advantage.

For better or worse, the members of the force are soldiers, not crafty politicians.

They're all fighting for the safety of their homes, so I was confident that with enough time, they would be won over by the hero's sincerity and character.

The force would be a perfect training ground for Sir Hero to learn to deal with adults before inevitably facing the slyest of them in the future, a major opportunity for his growth.

No doubt the ever-calculating Word of God pontiff considered all this when he appointed the young hero to the role.

Yes, at first, I watched over the hero like a parent might monitor their child's growth.

But I was still greatly underestimating the hero.

I was always working intently to destroy the human-trafficking organization—there's no doubt in my mind about that.

But Sir Hero's goal was something far more important.

From the very start, he had his eyes on the people.

And the goal of peace.

The young hero thought more intently than any of us about how to reduce the number of the organization's victims, and he worked hard to put that into action.

We adults and our petty problems were just background noise for him.

What Sir Hero cares about most of all is whether he can save people or not, and keeping pace with us would be nothing more than a hindrance to his goals.

I thought I was encouraging the hero's growth?

What a ridiculous, shameful misunderstanding that was.

The hero attains that role only because he is worthy of it.

Our Sir Hero's spirit is far past any opportunities for growth I might try to offer him.

No doubt he would sound naive to some, but his determination to strive for justice against all odds may be one of his greatest strengths.

As soon as I realized my own hubris, I immediately started taking action to correct it.

So that the force wouldn't hold Sir Hero back.

For the sake of saving people, not my personal grudge.

First, I needed the commanders to realize that they were only hindering Sir Hero.

At the same time, I put him on the front lines as he wished.

Sir Hero is meant to protect others, not to be protected himself.

Therefore, it would be pointless to deny him the chance to engage in life-and-death battles.

Yes, I regretted not sending guards with my son and his family.

But ultimately, my son, too, was a person meant to protect others.

He fought to protect his wife and son, even if he was regrettably unsuccessful.

As I watched Sir Hero, I began to realize that perhaps I should have been proud of my son for fighting rather than tormenting myself with regrets.

As the force made more progress, the men began to see Sir Hero with new eyes.

They looked at him as a warrior to be respected, not a child to be protected. As they should.

All of us had been taking the hero too lightly, myself included.

And I would soon learn that there was one other person I was still underestimating.

The Word of God pontiff.

He created this force purely as a place for Sir Hero to grow.

Not just so that he could experience clashing with adults, as I had thought at first.

So that he could experience real, physical battles.

And what's more, so that he could grow accustomed to taking the lives of others.

Prior generations of heroes were naturally exposed to fighting due to the war with the demons.

But now that the demons have stopped attacking, most people have less experience with that sort of combat.

Even the empire's soldiers are largely inexperienced, so of course a young boy like Sir Hero would never have fought in a real battle against his fellow man.

Whether one has killed before is very important in this sort of battle.

Even the most thoroughly trained soldier will hesitate to take a life for the first time. Very often, that moment of hesitation leads to their own deaths.

Demons look virtually indistinguishable from humans, but they are far stronger.

They're not a foe one can afford to hesitate against, even for the hero.

In order to battle demons, it's vital to have experience with taking the lives of other humans first.

The members of the human-trafficking organization make for a perfect opponent for Sir Hero to build up experience against, since felling them should cause little pain to the conscience.

Thus, Sir Hero must learn to kill, even at his young age.

If he is ever to fight demons, it will be a crucial strength for him.

So it is with some horror that I realize the pontiff must have factored all of this in his calculations.

I have no doubt that there are even more horrifying hidden truths behind the human-trafficking organization, which is shrouded in mystery.

The Word of God Church has designated it thus, as a "human-trafficking organization," but in reality, there are few instances of the captured victims being sold into slavery.

We know that some of the victims were actually bought and taken away somewhere, but we have no idea what happens to them.

Some have indeed been sold into slavery or even placed with new guardians, but given the total amount of vanished individuals, such instances represent a tiny minority.

The fate of the majority of the victims is unknown, and no bodies have been found.

Where in the world have these stolen victims been taken?

The state of the organization's hideouts varies greatly.

Some are on a vast scale, while others hide out in caves with very few members.

Common thugs kidnap people, and someone from the organization pays for them and takes them away.

In other words, what we generally deal with are bands of common criminals, not the human-trafficking organization itself.

We've yet to capture any actual members of the human-trafficking organization.

Their actions are bold and obvious, yet too skillful to leave any traces behind.

Considering how much space it would require to hold all these prisoners captive, there's no doubt that some nation or other is directly involved.

I suspected Sariella and did some investigating on my own, but I came up empty-handed.

Aside from the bases in Sariella, where we are not allowed to tread, we've crushed most of the organization's hideouts, yet we still don't have a full picture of the organization itself.

If Sariella was not behind it, I suspected the demons, but it was doubtful that the empire would let them take so many captives across the border so easily.

Considering the huge number of victims, it would be impossible to transport them without being noticed at some point.

Since the empire keeps a close eye on the border with the demon realm, I cannot imagine that anyone would miss something so obvious.

So we continue to crush the last of the bandits who have already been cut off from the organization, still devoid of any clues as to their greater identity.

If we finish crushing all of these criminal hideouts, I doubt we'll be able to chase down the organization any further.

There must be something, some important clue I'm missing.

But I have no idea what that might be.

I suspect that the pontiff knows, but of course he will not deign to tell us.

There must be something bigger at work here.

Something far beyond our understanding.

The day Sir Hero traveled back to his homeland, I was making preparations for our attack on the next human-trafficking-organization base.

Morale in the force was high.

Inspired by Sir Hero, the troops were determined to defeat the organization in order to protect innocent people.

Even without his presence, the others had the mettle to take the initiative and try to keep moving, something I never could have imagined when the force was first formed.

Sir Hero spoke of this as if it was all my doing, but the only thing I did was remove the obstacles hindering him, myself and the other leaders included.

All of this was thanks to Sir Hero's influence.

He hesitated over whether to go home, but I learned that it was for his younger siblings' Appraisal ceremony.

Given his strong sense of responsibility, I was sure he felt reluctant to take his leave while the rest of us are still working, but there was no need for him to worry about such things.

Even the most hardened warriors need a break occasionally, and he should be present for such a momentous family occasion.

…Especially since you never know when your family might be taken from you.

I felt that he should spend time with them as much as possible and create plenty of memories in the event that one of them might someday perish.

After losing my son and his family, I couldn't help dwelling on whether I could have made more time for them while they were still alive, so I do not want Sir Hero or his family to have the same regrets.

Not that I intend to let him die, of course.

But just like my son, there may come a day when the hero is defeated somewhere out of my reach.

Since he has chosen the battlefield, he has to live with the ever-present possibility of that fate.

"Sir Tiva."

As we prepared to attack, one of my subordinates ran up to me, the one generally in charge of gathering information.

"What is it?"

"Well, we've located an organization hideout nearby."

"Pardon?"

I could scarcely believe my ears.

Who would expect the human-trafficking organization to have a hideout so near the capital of the Holy Kingdom of Alleius, the seat of the Word of God religion?

To set themselves up right underneath the nose of our force's home base was brazen in the extreme.

But perhaps that was why we didn't find it sooner?

"How large?"

"It's hard to say, since we've only just found it, but most likely on the small side."

"I'm impressed you were able to locate it."

"Well, a citizen happened to witness a child being taken away in the immediate vicinity and contacted us."

"What?"

Did that mean the child was still being held in this base?

"When did this happen?"

"Earlier today, I'm told."

The human-trafficking organization was quick to retrieve kidnapped victims.

We didn't know what means they used to arrive so soon after the bandits captured someone.

Even the criminals themselves didn't seem to know how the organization representatives kept such a close eye on their activities.

Since the common criminals had no means of contacting the organization, we'd never been able to catch wind of their scent, but perhaps this was a one-in-a-million chance.

If we were lucky, we might be able to capture the organization member who came to retrieve the child.

Or at the very least, perhaps we could save the victim.

"We have twenty or so men who can move immediately."

If the hideout was a small one, then that should be more than enough to take care of it.

"Hmm…we don't have enough time to get permission. We're just going to have to act."

Even with a force that transcends borders, we aren't allowed to simply go on the attack in another nation without permission.

But this was an emergency situation, so they'd have to accept it.

If I went through the proper channels, we might not make it in time, even if we could have otherwise.

"Dispatch a messenger anyway."

"Yes, sir."

If we at least sent out an explanation right away, hopefully that would minimize the trouble later.

With that, I gathered all the men who were ready for immediate action, and we hurried to the newly located hideout.

This new hideout was one of the cavern types.

There were generally two types of hideouts that the criminals used: either areas like ghost towns and deserted houses or caverns like these.

The latter can be divided into two subcategories: natural caverns or caverns that were once home to monsters.

There are some monsters that dig holes and create subterranean burrows to live in.

These caves are usually considered nests or even small mazelike dungeons created by monsters.

Most likely, this particular cavern was created by monsters. Since it was an abrupt downward-slanting hole not far from a human settlement, I doubted it formed naturally.

The danger of these former monster nests was that it was impossible to know how large they were inside, and they often had complicated structures.

Monsters tended to make complex tunnels to fend off outside attackers.

And since they're underground caverns, they're generally too narrow to move in large groups easily.

"Is this the only entrance?"

"We believe so. We searched the surrounding area but didn't find anything else."

If this was truly the only entrance, then our targets couldn't escape as long as we kept it tightly locked down.

"We'll have seven men stay here. If anything happens, one of you should be ready to run with the message at a moment's notice."

There were twenty-two of us here, myself included.

I decided to leave a third of the group to watch the entrance and explore the cavern with the rest.

"Hmm?"

Suddenly, I turned around, feeling as though I was being watched.

But there was nobody there save for a small white bug.

Perhaps I was just on edge because of what we were about to do.

"Be sure to leave some space between yourselves and proceed so we don't hinder one another's movements."

As I gave these orders, I stepped into the cavern.

It was more spacious inside than I thought, so tight quarters shouldn't be a problem.

But if it was this large, I worried that there might be more criminals here than I'd expected.

We mustn't let our guards down.

But contrary to my expectations, we didn't run into a single soul as we proceeded deeper into the cavern. And there was only one long path, not a maze of tunnels.

Of course, fifteen fully equipped soldiers were bound to make noise, no matter how carefully we were proceeding.

Surely, they would have heard us, yet there was no sign of anyone coming to intercept us.

Had they run away?

Was there an exit that we didn't find?

Or were they gone before we even arrived?

As these thoughts raced through my mind, I suddenly felt as if my body had grown heavy.

And at the same time, a bright light flashed wildly from deeper in the cavern.

There was an ear-piercing sound, and I fell to the ground with no idea of what had happened.

"Nnngh!"

What in blazes was that?!

Looking forward, I saw that the soldiers in front of me had all fallen, too.

The ones farther ahead appeared to have died almost instantly.

Blood splattered everywhere, and in some cases, even a few limbs had gone flying.

The groans around me indicated that there were a few survivors, but not a one was unharmed.

"Hrm?"

As I took all this in, a lone man walked toward us, tilting his head curiously.

He held something long and black—not a sword but some new kind of weapon?

Was that what had annihilated our group in a matter of seconds?

"Knowing that man, I expected a clever trap or two. Perhaps I was overthinking it?"

The man murmured to himself in a level, emotionless voice.

How strange.

My hearing seemed much worse than usual.

And my wounds were taking far longer to heal.

Most disturbing of all, despite my Pain Mitigation skill, I was assaulted by such agony that I nearly writhed around on the ground.

What in the world was going on?

"I put up an Anti-Technique Barrier and used valuable bullets, yet there seem to be nothing but small fry here. What a waste."

The man scowled as he spoke.

Walking up to one of the wounded who lay still, groaning on the ground, he raised his foot and swiftly brought it down on the poor fellow's head.

As if he was squashing a bug.

He repeated this with each soldier as he moved through the group.

I knew I had to move, but my wounded body wouldn't obey me.

And as I struggled, soon it was my turn next.

I looked up at the man, who now stood almost directly over me.

His ears were longer and pointier than ours.

"An elf?"

A cold shock hit me like an avalanche.

The masterminds behind the human-trafficking organization, the mysterious nation, the location of the many disappeared victims that we could never find.

It all made sense.

I had ruled them out from the beginning, but there was one nation, one race that could make all of that happen.

The elves.

A race shrouded in mystery, who lived in a place known as the elf village, where humans were forbidden to trespass.

It's said that the entire elf race lives there, but they've been known to appear suddenly and unexpectedly in places all over the world, then disappear just as quickly.

If they were using those same methods to bring the captives to the elf village, that would explain everything.

And humans cannot enter the village, so of course we couldn't investigate.

And yet, the place must be large enough to host an entire race.

They could have easily hidden all the kidnapped victims there.

Who would have suspected that the elves were behind the human-trafficking organization?!

The nature-loving elves, who strive for world peace and lend their strength to charitable efforts?!

And the entire race was involved, at that!

"Lord Potimas Harrifenas. So you were behind all this?!"

"Hmm?"

I've seen this elf man before.

He's visited the empire as a delegate of the elves several times.

"…Ah. I recognize that face. You're from the empire…though I've forgotten your name."

Though I remember him well, Potimas doesn't recall exactly who I am. As if I was too trivial to be worth remembering.

I felt a tremor of humiliation.

"You were a man of some import, as I recall, but I can hardly let you live now that you've seen my face here."

As if he intended to let any of us live anyway!

With the last trace of my strength, I grabbed Potimas's leg.

"Damn you…damn you!"

I screamed at him, barely able to form a coherent sentence.

Without a doubt, this man was responsible for the deaths of my son and his family.

Not only that, but he was the cause of countless kidnappings and tragedies the whole world over.

He cannot be allowed to live.

If he does, he would surely only bring about even greater calamities.

And then Sir Hero would be in danger.

I tightened my grip on his leg as best I could.

But I could do no more and could only watch as Potimas looked down at me disinterestedly and raised his other foot.

Then the boot plunged down toward me.

Sir Hero.

My final thoughts were of my son and his family and the young hero's face.

Interlude   THE ELF DESPISES WASTING TIME

I crush the man's skull, silencing his irritating racket.

I seem to recall that he was an important figure to the empire, but I doubt killing him here will cause any serious problems.

Besides, given his age, he didn't have much time left anyway.

Probably twenty or thirty years at the most.

I just hurried the process along a little.

Still, though, this has been quite the letdown.

Our goal here was to acquire the reincarnation located in the Holy Kingdom of Alleius, the seat of the Word of God religion.

This is likely the last reincarnation we'll be able to abscond with.

The others, largely nobility and royalty, would be difficult to lay a hand on.

On top of that, thanks to the movements of this so-called anti-human-trafficking task force that includes humanity's hero, we've lost bases in many areas.

It wouldn't be impossible to capture the remaining reincarnations by force, but it would be quite risky.

Besides, we've already obtained a sufficient sample size of reincarnations, so I feel no need to go to unreasonable lengths to gather the rest.

The only reason I decided to go into the heart of enemy territory to try to capture this one is because I knew it was a trap.

That man, the pontiff of the Word of God, must have figured out the existence of the reincarnations by now.

He already has two of them under his thumb, at that.

So why would he refrain from collecting a third reincarnation so close to his home base, if not as a trap to lure me in?

If one knows of a trap from the start, it's easier to take measures accordingly.

Which is why I used this body, equipped with an Anti-Technique Barrier, and even brought along a precious gun.

So imagine my disappointment when I was met with a group of mere humans.

I was looking forward to seeing how much power he was willing to send out against me, though I suppose this is a measure of that.

Ah well.

I've acquired the reincarnation I was after.

If this was the best group they could send to attack me, perhaps the Word of God has little power left.

They must still be recovering from the G-Fleet incident that occurred four years ago, which significantly depleted the Word of God's military might.

I imagine that's why they gathered soldiers from other nations for the anti-human-trafficking force, as well.

I suppose acquiring this information counts as a win.

"Lord Potimas, preparations for our return are complete."

As I ruminate on all this, the disposable who's carrying the unconscious reincarnation arrives from deeper inside the cave.

"There may be a few more of them outside. Kill them all—don't let a single one get away."

"Yes, sir!"

Several of the disposables run toward the entrance at my orders.

Our work here is done.

There were never any organization pawns here to begin with.

It was just a temporary base for retrieving the reincarnation.

We lose nothing by abandoning it and leave nothing behind, especially not any proof that the elves were involved.

It's possible that the pontiff will manipulate public opinion and spread rumors of our involvement, but without proof, it will be easy to deny.

And as we have no further need to gather more reincarnations, the organization will make no more moves.

The extra humans we captured as a smoke screen have been processed as materials, too, allowing me to replenish what I lost in the G-Fleet incident.

Everything is going perfectly.

Now I merely have to wait for that foolish girl Ariel to make her move.

Nothing can stop me from progressing forward.

Yet, as I head to walk outside, I realize that something is still gripping my leg.

This man truly doesn't know when to give up, even in death.

I shake my foot lightly to rid myself of his hand, but it still doesn't let go.

Even when I stoop down to pull it free with my own hands, the man's fingers have already hardened too much to remove.

Rigor mortis?

So soon after death?

Impossible.

But what if the man's will made it so…?

Hmph. What a ridiculous notion.

Utterly unscientific.

Growing irritated, I fire a bullet at the man's wrist, detaching his hand from his body.

And yet, it still continues to cling to me.

Annoyed, I forcibly yank it off with all my strength and throw it to the ground.

Sophia's Diary 5

Ughhh, I'm soooo mad!

What is it this time, you ask?

It's that stupid Goody Two-shoes and the class rep girl!

Goody Two-shoes keeps getting all up in my business, like he's got something to prove!

Test scores, practical skill grades, and stuff like that—he's always trying to caaaasually check to see if he beat me.

Too bad I aaaalways come out on top!

Oh-ho-ho-ho-ho!

I'm a reincarnation, you loser!

I'm not going to be defeated by some snot-nosed kid!

So I always make a point of laughing right in his annoying face!

Serves him right!

What?

That doesn't sound very mature?

Oh, shut up.

But I guess that must have fanned the flames of his one-sided rivalry or something, because now he just sticks close to me around the clock.

It's super unsettling, like I'm being monitored twenty-four seven!

And if that wasn't annoying enough, there's Miss Class Rep, too!

She's not actually the class rep or anything, but that's what she reminds me of, so that's what I call her in my head.

Anyway, Miss Class Rep is apparently Mr. Goody Two-shoes's fiancée.

It's the first time I've ever heard someone actually use that word, let me tell you.

But either way, she told me to stop getting so close to a boy who has a fiancée.

He's the one who keeps getting too close to me, idiot!

Why am I the one to blame here?

Are you kidding me?!

Argh, I can't take it anymore!

And this cycle of stupidity continues every day!

I need more Merazophis in my diet.

So take this thread off me and let me run away already.

What do you mean you can't?

Jerk!

J6   JULIUS, AGE 13: LIFE AND DEATH

There was a group funeral for Mr. Tiva and the other twenty-one men who were killed.

They were the first of the special task force to die in the line of duty.

I'm sure no one expected Tiva to be among them, never mind that his entire squadron would be wiped out.

The pontiff conducted the funeral himself.

Instead of his usual gentle smile, he wore a bleak expression throughout.

To me, it looked like he really was grieving the deaths of Mr. Tiva and the others.

Even after the funeral ends, I stay seated in the temple for a while.

Yaana, Hyrince, and the others go outside, where the caskets are lined up.

Later, they'll be delivered to their respective homelands to be buried.

So now is my last chance to say my good-byes, but...I can't do it.

It still doesn't seem real to me that Mr. Tiva is gone.

I feel like I'm in a nightmare.

But I'm sure that once I see his casket, I'll be dragged into reality, whether I like it or not.

Right now, I'm too afraid of that to move.

I don't know how long I've been sitting here or how long someone's been next to me, but at some point, I notice his presence.

It's my teacher, Master Ronandt.

"Master...you're here."

"Indeed."

The empire is on a different continent from the Holy Kingdom of Alleius.

It'd be difficult to get here for most, but as one of the few people in the world who can use Space Magic, my master can teleport with ease.

They must have used a teleport gate to send word of Mr. Tiva's death to the empire, leading my master to come here in a rush.

"Nothing ever goes right, eh?"

Without meeting my eyes, Master speaks quietly, as if to himself.

"They keep dying before me, even though they're all younger. Though I suppose Tiva was getting up there in years himself. But then, why couldn't he stick it out a little longer and outlive me, dammit?"

Though his words are bitter, the usual fire is gone from his voice.

"Most of my comrades from the war with the demons are dead and gone. My dear friend the prior sword-king has vanished, so all that leaves is the swordsman and me. Tiva was a little younger than us, true, but he was one of the last survivors of the war."

Sounding inconsolable, Master heaves a long sigh.

"...Master, what sort of a person did Mr. Tiva seem like to you?"

For some reason, I can't help asking.

"Do you know what that fellow was called in the empire?"

"No..."

"The Savior in the Shadows."

Somehow, hearing that doesn't really surprise me.

I knew from experience just how amazing he was.

It doesn't shock me that people would call him a savior.

"The sword-king, the master swordsman, and me. We were the three who stood out most on the battlefield, but Tiva worked quietly but diligently where it mattered most, contributing to our victory. Some say the only reason we could fight fearlessly was because we knew he was supporting us in the shadows. So certain know-it-alls even like him better than us. Although I was more amazing, of course," he adds.

He wasn't flashy but was reliable enough that others could fight without fear or reservations.

That's exactly how Mr. Tiva seemed to me, too.

It was because of him that I was able to leap to the front lines.

And now we've lost our Savior in the Shadows.

"If only I had been there…," I murmur without thinking.

If I hadn't been at the Appraisal ceremony, if I had been at Mr. Tiva's side, maybe the results would've been different.

"If you had been there? Hah."

Master snorts.

"What's so funny?!"

I get angry despite myself.

But when I meet Master's eyes, my anger vanishes at once.

"What's so funny, you ask? All of it, of course."

His voice is trembling with the effort to conceal his rage.

He's angry, far angrier than I am.

But not at me.

I can't understand what's made him so angry, but I can tell that he's taking something else out on me.

"Of course. I haven't been much of a master lately. Perhaps it's time for some more training."

With that, he reaches out toward me abruptly before I can avoid it.

The intensity of his emotion has me rooted to the spot.

His hand grabs my shoulder.

At the same time, my vision darkens for a second, and suddenly we're not in the temple anymore.

We're in a wasteland, empty as far as the eye can see.

He must have taken me somewhere with teleportation.

But why?

"Now then, come at me as if you intend to kill me. Hrm, and I suppose I'll be half-serious with you, too."

Master takes a few steps away from me.

"Huh? Wait…"

"Well? I'll at least give you a head start. You're not going to take it?"

I still haven't quite grasped the situation, but…he's serious.

He intends to train me right here and now.

And with real combat, no less.

Master's training is incredibly harsh, to the point where my life has been in real danger several times in the past.

But in actuality, he's never once agreed to face me in single combat.

So why now?

"If you won't attack, then I will, boy. A real enemy wouldn't wait for you like this."

As I hesitate, Master produces his staff out of nowhere.

It's the Space Magic spell Space Storage, a spell that lets the user store items in an alternate dimension.

"Oh, right—I suppose you're unarmed. Very well, then. I'll give you one more handicap, eh?"

After the staff, Master pulls out a sword.

He tosses it to me, so I hurriedly catch it.

"Is this a magic sword?"

Pulling it out of the sheath, I see a remarkably high-quality blade.

When I charge it with magic, flames run along the edge.

"Indeed. A certain idiot forced a monster to mass-produce them."

"Mass-produced magic swords?"

I've never heard of such a thing.

It's incredibly difficult to produce magic swords, so even the most talented of blacksmiths can't make them easily.

So how could they be mass-produced?

"Well, that's not important right now. I'll lend that to you, so come at me."

"Do we really have to do this?"

"There'll be plenty of times when you have to fight even though you don't want to, child. Quit complaining and attack already."

Master doesn't seem willing to back down.

And I won't be able to return without his teleportation.

In the worst-case scenario, I might have to find my way out of this unfamiliar wasteland myself until Master comes around.

So I have no other choice.

"All right."

"Good."

I can't hold back if it's Master I'm fighting.

First, I'll feint with magic.

I create a Light Sphere with Holy Light Magic and fling it toward him.

At the same time, I charge at him with the sword in hand.

It would be foolish to try to engage in a long-distance battle with the strongest mage in the world.

If I have any chance of beating him, it's by shorten the distance between us and forcing a close-combat battle.

The only question is whether I can avoid his magic until then.

The Light Sphere crashes into Master's outstretched hand.

I assumed he would cancel it out with magic or avoid it, so my eyes widen in surprise.

Just as he said, he's giving me a head start as a handicap.

Without even blocking or dodging my attack.

It flashes into his palm—a direct hit.

But a moment later, he shakes out his hand as if nothing was ever there.

There's not a scratch on him.

He's wincing a little, but no more than if he had stubbed his toe.

It was only a feint, but I'm still shocked that he was able to take a direct hit from my magic with almost no damage at all.

Once again, I find myself questioning whether he's really human.

But in that instant, I was able to close the distance between us.

Even if my magic won't work, if my sword can reach, I have a chance!

"Hiyah!"

I swing down my sword with a shout, slicing through nothing but air.

Master is gone.

He literally transported away in an instant.

Space Magic is supposed to take a long time to use, but you'd never know from how quickly Master moved.

If he can get away from me with teleportation, then distance won't make a bit of difference.

Master could easily teleport far enough away that I can't reach him, then shoot magic at me from a long distance.

And even if I manage to cover that distance, he can just teleport away again.

I never had a chance to begin with.

But Master reappears far closer to me than I expected, perhaps because this is supposed to be training.

Right behind me.

Only about ten steps away—fairly close.

But those ten steps are much too far when fighting against Master.

He raises his staff.

Here it comes!

I jump to the side as fast as I can.

Immediately after, flames roar through the area where I was standing seconds before.

Any ordinary person would've likely been burned away to the bone.

Most frightening of all, that was just a beginner spell, Fireball.

Usually, the power of a spell doesn't differ much depending on who uses it.

High stats might make it a bit more powerful, but it wouldn't be a big enough difference to be visible at a glance.

Even if the caster's stats were ten times higher than average, that wouldn't make the spell ten times more powerful. It's traditionally more of an indicator of whether they can use more advanced spells.

If someone's stats are around a certain amount, then they'll likely be able to use a corresponding level of magic.

In some cases, if a person's stats are too low, a spell might backfire even if the user knows the skill.

Magic stats are a quick way to understand that—or at least they were.

Unfortunately, Master has rendered that knowledge completely useless.

With his stats that defy logic, he's figured out a way to use more magic power than necessary for previously known spells, increasing the power of the spell itself.

With this new breakthrough, now one's magic stats really can determine how strong a spell will be.

And of course, Master has the highest magic stats of anyone in the world.

In his hands, even beginner spells are far stronger than a massive magic spell unleashed by an entire group of lesser mages!

Even my Holy Magic barrier wouldn't be able to block it completely.

And yet...

"Ah!"

As I dodge the Fireball, Master's staff swivels to point toward me.

Yes, Fireball is a beginner spell.

Even with its power increased, it's still quick to use and requires little energy.

In other words, he can use it at a breakneck rate!

I break into a run.

A wave of heat hits my face, evaporating my sweat.

Am I sweating from the heat or from pure fear? Even I can't say for sure.

All I know is that if I stop moving, my entire body will be engulfed in flames.

So I keep pumping my legs as fast as I can to dodge his spells.

But running around like this isn't enough.

Just as I thought earlier, if I have any chance of winning, it's by forcing a close-combat battle.

I have to get closer to him somehow, or I won't even have that slim chance.

I shoot a Light Sphere at the next Fireball that comes my way.

The nodules of magic crash into each other, exploding with a roar.

Canceling each other out—or not quite.

My magic is pushed back a little, so the explosion flies in my direction.

He's overtaken an advanced Holy Light Magic spell, the weapon of the hero, with a beginner's spell.

What an amazingly powerful person.

But I managed to get one step closer to him by using the Light Sphere to deflect his magic.

One down, nine to go!

I jump into the air to avoid the blast.

Another Fireball comes flying toward me in midair.

Now!

I use a skill—Dimensional Maneuvering!

An invisible foothold forms below my feet, and I use it to jump off and dodge the Fireball.

Master's Fireballs move quickly and create a larger explosion when they hit their target.

If they hit their target.

He's been blanketing the surrounding area in flames by aiming his attacks at me on the ground, but he can't do that if I'm in the air.

And no matter how fast they might be, they're not impossible to dodge if I know they're coming.

But I'm still inexperienced with the Dimensional Maneuvering skill, and the same move won't work on Master twice, so this was a one-time-only strategy.

Still, that's two more steps now.

Between the one I gained first and the two from Dimensional Maneuvering, that leaves seven more steps!

As soon as I land on the ground, another Fireball comes flying toward me.

I deflect his Fireball with my own magic again, resulting in another shock wave.

But I reduce it with my barrier and take another step forward.

Six steps left!

I jump to the side to dodge the next Fireball.

At the same time, I use my ace-in-the-hole spell.

"Hrmmm?!"

Master exclaims for the first time since the fight started.

To him, it should look like there are suddenly three of me.

It's an illusion created with Light Magic.

I run forward along with the two fakes from three different directions.

Even Master can't shoot a spell in three directions at the same time—at least, I hope not.

"Aren't you tricky."

A Fireball shoots out and hits one of the three.

But the other two keep running toward him without slowing down.

Five more steps.

Another Fireball strikes the second one.

Four more steps.

"You're the real one, eh? You got lucky."

A third Fireball hits the last one standing.

"What?!"

Then Master exclaims in genuine confusion for the first time.

Three more steps.

Master freezes in surprise for only a second.

But that second buys me yet another step.

Two steps left!

"But how?!"

To tell the truth, the first Fireball actually hit the real me.

Master commented that I was lucky, but I was anything but in this case.

No, I guess it was probably my master's impeccable instincts rather than luck.

I'm sure he saw through the fakes in an instant and shot at the real me on purpose.

But when the other two kept moving after that one was hit, he must have assumed that he'd been mistaken.

Even when I took a direct hit, I kept moving the two fakes forward.

And while he was distracted by them, I closed in.

I decided to take the Fireball without dodging because I figured I could withstand one direct hit.

Honestly, I regret it—it was very hot and painful, and still is.

But in exchange, I bought myself this chance.

I can't let it go!

"Take this!"

A Fireball shoots toward me at point-blank distance.

I don't have any way to dodge it, but...

"Yaaah!"

I charge the borrowed magic sword, cloaking it in flame.

Then I swing the sword to deflect the Fireball.

The flames of the spell and the sword clash, igniting a massive explosion.

It burns! I can't breathe!

But I have to keep moving forward!

Just one more step!

"Huh?"

I blurt out a foolish exclamation.

I thought I had one step left to go.

But before I take it, Master is already standing in front of me.

"Did you think you could win if you got close enough to me?"

His staff swings down on me.

It's so unexpected that I react too late.

It wasn't particularly fast, but the staff attack still strikes me right in the face.

The pain is nothing compared to that Fireball, but I still stumble backward.

That proves to be my undoing.

A Fireball nails me.

The next thing I know, I'm looking up at the sky.

"Well?"

"I was just one step away..."

I grumble without really thinking.

"Don't be stupid. If I was fighting seriously, it would've been over before you even took a single step."

Of course. Master was actually still holding back.

He used only Fireballs, and even those were restrained enough that a direct hit didn't instantly kill me.

"Do you now realize how weak you are, boy?"

"...Yes."

I still can't come anywhere near beating Master.

Considering that he used Teleport only that one time, I'm sure I wouldn't have won even if I had closed those ten steps.

If he really felt he was in danger, he could've easily teleported away again.

"Listen, Julius. Was Tiva weak?"

"No!" I exclaim immediately.

"But this enemy was still able to kill him easily. If you were there, the only difference would be one more dead body."

"Maybe, but—"

"Let me ask you again. Do you realize how weak you are?"

This time, I can't bring myself to answer.

Because I realize now just how deep the weakness he's speaking of goes.

Even now, I'm sure I don't fully understand it.

"Tiva fought someone stronger than himself and lost. That's all there is to it. Just like the thrashing I gave you a moment ago."

I chew the inside of my lip as he goes on.

"Do you understand? The weak can never defeat the strong. You told me Tiva wasn't weak. To you, I'm sure he didn't seem that way. But the person he fought was even stronger than he was. That's it."

"You only say that so easily because *you're* strong, Master!"

Of course Master wouldn't lose.

He's the strongest living human mage. Who could beat him?

But Master's response catches me by surprise.

"No. I am weak. I might seem strong to you, but I'm still weak."

At first I think he must be joking, but his expression is deadly serious.

"Listen closely, Julius. Humans are weak. Incredibly weak. Most humans are even weaker than I am, which is why they look at me and say that I'm strong. But I'm only human, too. I'm strong by human standards, but that's all."

These are the words of the strongest human mage.

"You know this, too, do you not? You've seen true strength. The Nightmare of the Labyrinth."

The words bring to mind a hellish memory.

A battlefield in chaos, where people on both sides were dying nonstop.

The creature that appeared at the battle of Sariella and Ohts, the one called the "Nightmare," was the personification of death itself.

"You mean even you couldn't beat it, Master?"

"I think not. The difference between my strength and that master's is even vaster than that between yours and mine."

I couldn't lay a finger on Master in our fight, and he says he wouldn't be able to beat the Nightmare.

"Apprentice number one. You must come to grips with your own weakness. Know that there are some foes in this world that humans cannot touch, even the hero. You must learn to recognize that some things are impossible."

In a way, those words are incredibly painful.

I've been through near-death experiences at Master's hands many times, including our fight just now.

But somehow, his words are even more painful.

"Then what am I supposed to do?! Why did I...? Why did Mr. Tiva have to...? Why?!"

Even I don't know what I was trying to say.

Maybe the words didn't have any meaning at all.

My grief over Mr. Tiva's death was simply spilling out of my mouth.

Abruptly, I realize there are tears streaming from my eyes.

"There are many things in this world we can do nothing about. But we still must live as best we can. There was nothing we could do about Tiva's death, but he lived with all his might. If you sit around bemoaning the impossible, you cheapen Tiva's life, you know."

"But…!"

"For now, don't worry about anything. Just let it out."

Master embraces me gently, patting my head.

Unable to hold back any longer, I sob into his chest.

"People live and someday die. We cannot change that. Nor can we choose how we will die. But what we *can* choose is how we live. It's not how he died that's important but how he carried himself in life. Thinking about what you can do for the dead, what you could've done for the dead, is nothing but a form of arrogance. All the living need do is grieve the dead and remember how they lived."

After I cried for a while, Master brought us back to the temple, and we said our final good-byes to Mr. Tiva at his casket.

There were others pressing close to the casket with their eyes reddened like mine, including Yaana and Aurel, the apprentice Master took on after me.

"Master?"

"Hrmmm?"

"I want to live like Tiva did, in a way that people will cry for me when I die."

"Then go ahead. You have every freedom to do so."

"Right."

"But remember to learn your own weakness first. If you can't discern between what you can and can't do, you'll just recklessly hasten your death. There's no point living the way you wish if you don't live long."

"Yes, sir."

"Although I can't help feeling that you're going to be reckless anyway."

"I won't."

"Hrm. All right, this is an order from your master. You are forbidden to die before me. Understand? And when I die, you have to cling to my casket and cry even harder than you did today."

"Um, I don't know…"

"Hey, what's that supposed to mean?"

"Nothing."

I can't tell him that I can't imagine him ever dying, and definitely not that I don't think I'd be able to cry even more than I just did.

But if that day ever does come, I'm sure I will cry at least as much as I did today.

"I just hope that day never comes," I say instead.

"It will. People die sooner or later. The only way you won't see that day is if you disobey my order. And you wouldn't want to be a useless apprentice who doesn't even follow his master's orders, eh?"

"Right. Of course."

That day, Mr. Tiva taught me about death, and Master taught me how to live.

Deep in my heart, I vowed to live as heroically as Mr. Tiva did, until the day I die.

Interlude
The Pontiff and the Reincarnation Spy

"Testing, testing, one-two-three. Hello? Can you hear me, Pontiff?"

"Yes, I can."

"Nice! Looks like step one is a success, then."

"Indeed. It appears that your Unlimited Telephone skill is capable of connecting for conversation even through the elves' irritating barrier."

"Guess that's a unique skill for ya. I gotta say, I thought it was a pretty lame skill at first, but it's actually pretty impressive."

"Well, it is your special privilege as a reincarnation. It was bound to be an exceptional skill."

"So I succeeded in getting caught by the elves on purpose and infiltrating their village. Now what's the plan?"

"You will live there normally with the other reincarnations. Please contact me on a regular basis so you can report what's going on inside."

"You got it."

"I'm sincerely sorry to give you such a dangerous role."

"Nah, don't worry about it. I'm cooperating with you of my own free will. It just happens to be the best way to save my friends, that's all."

"Well, please do be careful. Until the day we come there ourselves, we cannot interfere with what goes on inside. It's best you assume that no one will be able to help you, no matter what happens."

"Yeah, I know. I'll be extra careful so it doesn't come to that."

"Thank you."

"Oops, looks like we're about out of phone time. I'll contact you again soon."

"Very well. Be careful."

With that, the call ends.

The person on the other end was the reincarnation who was recently captured by the elves.

I had him deliberately let the elves catch him so that he can be our spy on the inside of the elf village, sending us information on a regular basis.

It's all possible thanks to his Unlimited Telephone skill.

Just as I hoped, it works even through the barrier that protects the elf village, unlike regular telepathy.

As our agent on the inside, he'll be in some danger, but now I finally have a means of knowing what goes on in the elf village.

It's been my dearest wish for many long years to defeat the elves, specifically Potimas.

Thus far, the barrier around their home has always prevented me from even coming close.

We've found several of the teleport gates that the elves utilize to travel in and out, but those can transport only a few people at a time.

There'd be no chance of a successful invasion with such low numbers.

And after we'd used a teleport gate once, the elves would be sure to destroy it, so we could never use it again.

No, it was important to wait for our chance to launch an all-out attack on the elf village.

But time dragged on without such a chance ever arising. I never even had any way to get inside information about their homeland.

Now, I don't know why Potimas is confining reincarnations in the elf village.

But whatever the reason, it finally created a chance to secret people other than elves into the elf village.

I do not know if this will lead to an opportunity for an all-out attack, but it will certainly allow me to keep a better eye on their activities.

…However, I never imagined the cost of getting him into the elf village would be so high.

To think that we would lose Sir Tiva…

A villager happened to see our reincarnation being kidnapped and reported it to Sir Tiva.

And the man has always been quick to act.

If Sir Tiva had only hesitated over his decision a little longer, I might have been able to slow him down and perhaps prevent this outcome.

But he made a swift decision and dived into action immediately.

Ironically, it was his exceptional leadership that caused this tragedy.

Without Sir Tiva, the heart of their military, the empire will fall into chaos.

The anti-human-trafficking force, too, was held together by Tiva. It will be difficult to keep that going for much longer now.

Fortunately, they've already succeeded in crushing all the major bases of the organizations.

Potimas has made little movement since then, too.

Once they destroy the next base, all that will be left are small-time bandit groups that could easily be handled by local knights and such.

I suppose then it will be best to disband the force.

The hero has matured quite nicely, too.

He's still far from being a match for Lady Ariel, but that is inevitable. No hero could ever compare to her.

However, he shall at least need to become strong enough to defeat an average demon.

Lady Ariel is an ally when it comes to the fight against Potimas, but at the end of the day, she is still the Demon Lord and an enemy in her own right.

Potimas and Lady Ariel alike are far beyond the means of most any human.

Yet somehow, we have to face them.

It is all for the sake of humanity's survival.

For that is the sole reason for my existence.

Sophia's Diary 6

Ughhh, I'm sooooooo mad!
  Hmm?
  What's this?
  A bone?
  What about it?
  You want me to gnaw on it?
  What, to get some calcium?
  Um, no, I think I'll pass on that.
  H-hey!
  Don't give me those puppy-dog eyes!
  All right already!
  You just want me to gnaw on it, yeah?!
  Hrmmm? It's surprisingly soft, actually.
  It's not particularly tasty, but it's not inedible, either.
  …Hey, you're the one who gave it to me. Why do you look so disturbed?

J7   Julius, Age 13: Progress

It's been several days since we held a funeral for Mr. Tiva and the others.

Our force has set out on its final mission.

Mr. Tiva, who was really what held the force together, is gone, and this is the last major organization base that we've found. For these reasons, the pontiff has announced that the force will be disbanded after this mission.

There are still many mysteries surrounding the human-trafficking organization, and we don't know where most of the kidnapped victims have gone.

But it would be difficult to keep searching at this point, and since we've destroyed most of the bases, there shouldn't be any more victims in the future.

We're not satisfied with that conclusion, of course.

But somewhere in the organization is the villain who killed Mr. Tiva.

Just as my master said, I'm not strong enough to defeat that person right now.

Even if I was to stubbornly insist on chasing down the organization, I'd only die a pointless death if I wound up facing off against that person.

So instead, I just have to do whatever I can.

And that first step is the force's final mission.

We gained control over the last base easily.

The force's motivation was higher than ever, not least because it was a chance to avenge Tiva and the other soldiers who lost their lives.

And the enemy's morale was strangely low.

When we interrogated some of the captured bandits afterward, we learned it was because the organization representatives had suddenly stopped coming.

Normally, when the bandits capture someone, an organization person will appear out of nowhere and take the victim away, giving the criminals money or goods in exchange. But now that they stopped showing up, the criminals weren't getting paid, which hurt their morale.

The organization must have decided to stop their kidnapping activities.

So while we weren't able to figure out the source of the organization, there won't be any more kidnappings.

Although, since we never found out where the people who've already been captured were taken, it's hard to call this a draw.

However, as a silver lining, we were at least able to rescue the people who were captured by the last base. Since the organization members never came to get them, they were simply being held there.

Fortunately, they weren't treated too poorly, in case the organization came to pick them up.

We'd managed to save people in the process of destroying bases a handful of times before, but this was a much higher number than usual.

When we brought them back to their home villages and towns, their family and friends wept and embraced them.

For all the time I spent on this force, that was what I wanted to see more than anything else.

It took until the very last mission, but when I was finally able to see that and know that we'd saved someone, I quietly cried tears of relief.

When we returned to the Holy Kingdom of Alleius, we were promptly treated to a celebratory banquet.

It was a modest affair, held only with the force members and their families. The pontiff kindly provided the hall for us.

There was plenty of food and drink for all, and the force ate and drank without reserve, savoring every morsel.

Once this banquet ended, the soldiers would all go back to their respective homelands.

This jumbled mix of people from different nations would probably never be gathered in one place again.

So they all cut loose and celebrated to their hearts' content.

Although unfortunately, since Hyrince, Yaana, and I aren't old enough to drink, we couldn't quite keep up with everyone's enthusiasm.

Still, it was fun.

At the peak of the excitement, as more and more people drink themselves under the table, a man sits down across from me.

"It's over, eh?"

"Yes."

It's Mr. Jeskan, the adventurer.

He's had a considerable amount of liquor himself, but the only effect I can see is a slight redness in his cheeks.

"Oh, where's Mr. Hawkin?"

"Ah, he's passed out drunk over there somewhere."

Mr. Jeskan points across the room, where a group of drunks are piled unconscious on top of one another.

How in the world did that happen?

And I don't see Mr. Hawkin in there anywhere. Is he underneath them?

"Won't he get crushed under there?" says Hyrince, aghast. "Physically speaking, I mean."

"Ha-ha-ha! He was a famous thief, despite all appearances. He's not soft enough to get crushed that easily."

Mr. Jeskan chuckles.

"So, Mr. Hero, the force is disbanding as of today. What will you do after this?"

"…I think I'm going to travel to different places and try to help people who are in trouble."

I saw many different nations in my time with the force, but the human-trafficking organization and their thugs weren't the only cause of people's suffering.

Monsters, poverty, discrimination, dangerous environments…

They all had different problems, but in one way or another, we never saw a single place that you could truly call peaceful.

"I know there probably isn't much that I can do. Most of their problems are probably beyond me. But still, I want to do whatever I can to help people."

"How admirable...!"

Yaana clasps her hands together and gazes at me emotionally.

"Very admirable, indeed."

Jeskan chuckles as he repeats Yaana's remark.

However, unlike Yaana, I can't help feeling like he's making fun of me a little.

"Excuse me, is there something you'd like to say to Sir Hero?!" Yaana demands of him indignantly.

"My hometown was destroyed by bandits."

At this sudden declaration, Yaana falls back with a gasp.

"It was a tiny settlement with just a few families, so small you could barely even call it a village. I didn't want to spend my whole life in a place like that, so I ran off and became an adventurer when I was still a kid."

Jeskan takes a gulp of his drink as he tells us about his past.

"The rest wasn't exactly dramatic. I heard through the grapevine that my hometown had been attacked by bandits who slaughtered everyone and stole every last item worth a damn. Not like I hunted down those bandits and got my revenge or anything, either. By the time I heard about it, some other adventurer had already found their stronghold and wiped 'em out."

"That's, erm...that must have been awful."

"Nah, not really."

Yaana offers her sympathies, but Mr. Jeskan lightly shakes his head.

"A shabby place like that with no defenses was bound to get destroyed by monsters or bandits eventually. That's why I ran off in the first place. When I heard it was gone, all I really thought was *Yeah, that doesn't surprise me.*"

Looking shocked, Yaana opens her mouth, but Jeskan continues.

"But I did learn something that day: People are evil deep down. They'll be as ruthless as they have to be to save their own skin. That goes for the robbers who destroyed my hometown—they were willing to murder and steal for their own sakes. And it goes for me, too. I abandoned my home so that I could survive. And even when it was destroyed, I didn't feel a thing."

Mr. Jeskan speaks without a hint of sarcasm, as if he's simply stating the truth.

"You saw the guys our force was fighting, didn't you? They had the same blood that runs in our veins. But they did things so heartless that it was easy to forget."

The people we were fighting are human just like us.

Sure, our circumstances are different, but we're all people.

In other words, if our positions had been reversed, we might've walked the same path of evil—because we're all only human.

"People aren't as noble as we'd like to think. But you still want to use your power to try to help them, Mr. Hero?"

Jeskan turns to me.

I already know the answer.

"Of course."

I've decided to live my life in a way I can be proud of.

I want to be a noble person like Mr. Tiva, the kind of person people will mourn when I die.

Quietly, I touch my scarf.

"I learned in my time with the force how easily people can turn to the path of evil, too. But that's exactly what my power is for."

Humans stain their hands with evil deeds all too easily.

So I just have to make sure it doesn't come to that.

"I am the hero, a symbol of hope for the people. An emblem of justice. And the enemy of evil. I'll become the hope of humanity and show them that I'll never let evil win."

"So you'll stop evil from ever happening?"

"Yes."

"Do you really think that's possible?"

"I won't know until I try. But I certainly won't give up before I've even started. If people have grown anxious because the previous hero hid himself away, then it's my job as the current hero to quell their fears."

"So you're cleaning up the last guy's mess?"

"I am here. I am the hero. That's what I want to let everyone know. As long as I do that, I'm sure the future will be full of hope."

"Ha...ah-ha-ha-ha! What a gem!"

Mr. Jeskan bursts out laughing, as if he can't hold it back any longer.

But this time, it doesn't sound like he's making fun of me at all.

"So this is the hero! Yeah, I get it now. You're the hero, all right!"

He bangs his glass on the table a few times as his laughter continues.

"...Hey, Sir Hero."

Then, when the laughter finally subsides, Mr. Jeskan looks at me.

And calls me "Sir Hero."

He was calling me "Mr. Hero" up until now, so I feel as if this means he's gained a new respect for me.

"I happen to know a skilled adventurer and a thief who're out of a job as of today. Any chance you'd be interested in hiring 'em?"

"You mean..."

"Oh, right, the pay. How about we call it even for the right to see this hopeful future you're talking about at your side?"

Mr. Jeskan grins at my surprised expression and raises his glass toward me.

I break into a smile and hold out my own cup to meet his.

"I believe we have a deal."

"That's what I like to hear."

I've gotten a good idea of Mr. Jeskan's and Mr. Hawkin's character through our time together in the task force.

At a glance, Mr. Jeskan might seem cynical and pragmatic, but moments like this show that he has a sense of justice and adventure deep down.

And as a former gentleman thief who stole for the sake of the poor, Mr. Hawkin is just as kind as his past would suggest.

Mr. Tiva once told me that I should gather companions who I can trust.

And I know I can trust Mr. Jeskan and Mr. Hawkin.

If they're willing to join forces with me, I could wish for nothing better.

Thus, I gain two trustworthy new companions.

Incidentally, Mr. Hawkin learned of all this while he was recovering from a hangover and made his own headache worse by shouting in surprise.

Sophia's Diary 7

Mm, bones!

Yeah, a girl could get addicted to this crunchy texture.

It even helps me feel a little less annoyed, or at least I'd like to think so.

Okay, that's probably not true.

Goodness, what is wrong with those idiots?!

I understand Miss Class Rep, okay?

It's her fiancé, after all.

I'd be steaming mad, too, if my fiancé was all over another girl.

But why are all the other girls so eager to jump on the bandwagon and bully me?!

What, because I've got a monopoly on the beloved idol of the class?

Yeah, right!

He's the one who keeps bothering ME!

I don't want anything to do with him, okay?!

I'm not interested in little kids!

Come back when you're at least as tall and handsome as Merazophis!

Of course, that's impossible, since Merazophis is the most handsome man in the world.

Ugh, I need more Merazophis time.

! Aha!

Mwa-ha-ha-ha!

I dodged it!

I finally dodged that damn thread!

I always, *always* get taken down with the first shot, but I finally dodged it!

Hey, wait a second!

I know it's always been one against three, but it's not fair if you team up on me from three different directions!

Stop that! Aaaah!

...Hey, isn't this pattern basically rope bondage?

I don't even want to know where you learned th... No, never mind, I guess there's only really one possible culprit.

Why would she teach them something like that?!

And why does this sort of thing keep happening to me?!

Seriously, unbelievable!

J8 Julius, Age 14: Youth

"Yaaaah!"

Jeskan swings his ax down with a shout, lopping off the tentacle that was stretching toward him.

"Boss!"

Hawkin turns to help Jeskan, but his master shouts out to stop him.

"I'm fine! Stay close to Miss Yaana!"

"Hey! Yaana, stay behind me, no matter what!"

"Wehhh, okay!"

Yaana cowers behind Hyrince's shield, her mouth drawn tightly.

"Ah!"

I cut down another tentacle, but they keep coming no matter how many we slice off.

We're fighting a monster called a Boellero, which has long, snakelike tentacles. The seemingly endless tentacles attack with paralyzing barbs on the end; then it devours its helpless prey.

And for some reason, this monster especially prefers to attack young women.

So the tentacles keep shooting toward Yaana, the lone girl in our midst.

Hyrince blocks the tentacles with his shield, while Hawkin covers him.

As Yaana keeps the monster's attention on her, Jeskan and I attack its main body.

At least, that was the plan—but it's turning out to be tougher than expected.

The tentacles grow back as fast as we can cut them off, making it all but impossible to deal a finishing blow.

The core of the Boellero is a sphere, and the larger it is, the higher-level and more dangerous the monster will be.

The Boellero we're fighting right now has a core easily twice the size of a human.

Considering that the average Boellero has a core around the size of a human head, that's unbelievably large.

"How many humans must it have eaten to get so big?!"

Jeskan groans as he slices off another tentacle.

"No wonder the adventurers' guild gave up on this thing!"

Defeating this Boellero was originally a job posted for members of the adventurers' guild.

But all the adventurers they sent to fight it were soundly defeated, so now it's fallen to us instead.

Adventurers make their living by defeating monsters and receiving reward money from the adventurers' guild. If we were to stick our noses in and defeat all those monsters, we'd be depriving adventurers of their livelihood.

In order to avoid that, we only deal with monsters too strong for the local adventurers to handle or other special cases where the adventurers' guild requests our involvement directly.

Which means that most of the requests that come our way are extraordinarily dangerous.

"Eeeek!"

Yaana screams and unleashes a Light Sphere spell toward the Boellero, but it's thwarted by another tentacle before it reaches the core.

The stricken tentacle grows back at an astounding rate.

"Idiot! Stay behind us!"

"Aaaah!"

The tentacle rushes toward Yaana, but Hyrince jumps in front of her and blocks it with his shield.

His shield is large enough to cover his entire body, which is already large for his age.

Since we added the attacker Jeskan to our roster, Hyrince has chosen to become a defender, focusing on the shield instead of the sword.

Now he protects our healer, Yaana, and our supporter, Hawkin, with that shield.

"Not so fast!"

One of the tentacles tries to go around Hyrince's shield to get at Yaana, but Hawkin's knife slices it off.

Hawkin doesn't boast as much battle power as most of us, but he's definitely not weak.

He's an expert in throwing knives, and I've been saved by a well-timed throw of his many times.

But Hawkin's real value lies outside of battle.

His main role is supporting us in other ways, like getting supplies, gathering information, and formulating plans based on what he's seen and learned.

He even hires bag carriers or pack animals for our luggage so that we can save our strength for battle.

It might sound like a modest job, but we can fight to the best of our ability only thanks to Hawkin.

Something about the way he works reminds me of Mr. Tiva.

"Hrm?! Tch!" Jeskan notices something and clicks his tongue. "An acid attack! My weapon's ruined!"

Without any further hesitation, he flings the ax in his hand at the Boellero's core.

It's blocked by tentacles, of course.

But as it hits the floor, the ax emits a strange smoke, and the blade starts melting away.

"This thing can use acid, too?!"

Acid Attack is a dangerous skill that can destroy weapons and armor.

Equipment enhanced with the Energy Conferment skill doesn't break easily, but an Acid Attack can damage it regardless.

Not only that, but it has its own unique resistance, so inexperienced adventurers who aren't used to it can easily take a large amount of damage from the attribute.

"Try not to touch the mucus on the tentacles! It'll melt right through!"

"Easy for you to say!"

Hyrince is desperately defending Yaana with his shield from the attacking tentacles.

He doesn't have a moment to spare to worry about the mucus.

On closer inspection, his shield is emitting the strange smoke that Jeskan's ax did.

This is bad.

We probably have a little longer before the thick shield breaks, but there's not a moment to waste.

"Guys! Buy me a little time, please!"

"Got it!"

"Understood!"

Jeskan and Hyrince call out their acknowledgments immediately.

It's been over a year since the anti-human-trafficking force was disbanded.

We've been traveling together to different nations, defeating monsters, taking down bandit hideouts the task force missed, and so on.

I think our teamwork has gotten very strong in the course of the past year.

Jeskan and I attack on the front lines, Yaana and Hawkin support us from the rear, and Hyrince stays in the middle to fend off attacks from the enemy depending on the situation.

Early on, I often had to depend on the older Jeskan, but lately, we've been in better sync.

We've even gotten closer off the battlefield and have started calling each other by name without any titles.

Knowing my dependable companions, I'm sure they'll buy me the time I need!

Jeskan pulls out a spare scimitar and starts lopping off more tentacles.

A master of many weapons, he always carries several at any given time and can swap them out as needed. His ax is no longer usable, but he still has plenty of other weapons.

However, the situation is looking grim.

The hole I left in the front lines is difficult for Jeskan and Hyrince to completely cover.

Hawkin and Yaana are trying to back them up, but it's obviously not enough.

"This is gonna put us in the red, but ya can't make an omelet without breakin' some eggs!"

Hawkin flings something toward the Boellero.

Whatever it is, it immediately explodes, freezing the tentacles over.

"Ha-ha! How d'ya like that?! Ice Bombs ain't cheap, but it was worth it!"

A disposable magic item?!

One-use-only magic items like that are very expensive, primarily because there aren't many artisans who can make them.

In exchange, though, their power is guaranteed.

The item Hawkin threw must have had an Ice Magic effect.

"○☆#%%!"

The Boellero emits an ear-piercing shriek.

Its tentacles flail around wildly as it writhes in pain.

I can't let this chance pass me by!

"Now!"

I unleash the spell I was forming in the time my friends bought for me: the Holy Light Magic spell Holy Light Spear.

Enhanced with extra magic power, just like Master taught me!

At my level of power, it takes me a while to create the spell, but Holy Light Magic is already powerful on its own, so it's even more so when imbued with extra strength.

The Holy Light Spear forces its way past the tentacles easily and pierces the core!

Then the entire area fills with a burst of light.

"Good work, everyone."

After completing the request, we gather to celebrate.

"Cheers!"

"""Cheers!"""

Jeskan and Hawkin toast with beer, the rest of us with fruit-flavored water.

"Ahhh… I never want to fight a Boellero again." Yaana sips her drink and sighs deeply, unable to hide the disgust in her voice. "Just thinking about it gives me goose bumps."

"Was it that bad? We didn't really notice anything."

"Of course it was!"

Yaana waves her glass at Hyrince, splashing a bit of fruit water.

"What are you saying? That repulsive creature was directing some horrible desires toward me. It was absolutely awful!"

Watching her tremble, I can't help but feel like we wronged Yaana by bringing her along.

Boelleros are supposed to be one of the three greatest enemies to women in the world.

It's said that their female victims are subjected to unspeakable things until they draw their last breath. Men are eaten immediately, yet women are kept alive.

There are rumors that some perverts like this horrible aspect of the creatures and will keep pet Boelleros in secret, deliberately supplying them with women.

Although in most cases, the would-be owners will fail to tame them and wind up eaten themselves.

Maybe the Boellero we fought escaped from similar circumstances.

Of course, I'm not interested in that kind of thing at all.

As a man myself, I guess I can see the appeal, but I would never say that and upset Yaana further.

"Why do such perverted things have to exist in this world? I wish it would all be destroyed!"

Clearly, she was so upset by the Boellero's evil intentions that she's saying some extreme things now.

"What are you talking about? If it wasn't for perversion, none of us would be born. You realize you're denying the reason you were made in the first place, right?"

Hyrince sounds shocked, but there's a smirk at the corners of his lips.

He's obviously teasing Yaana.

"That's not true! Don't compare the intercourse between a man and a woman in love with such foul proclivities. Love is far more sacred and noble!"

"PFFT!" Yaana's exclamation makes Hawkin spit out the beer he was sipping.

He starts to cough and choke, so Jeskan claps him on the back a few times.

I know there's no one else here except us, but I still don't think it's appropriate to shout about things like "intercourse" so loudly.

Yaana turns bright red, belatedly realizing the same thing.

"Yeah? So what specifically does this sacred and noble activity involve? Please teach us, O Great Saint."

"Th-th-th-that's—! That's not!"

Ahhh, she's playing right into Hyrince's hands again.

Poor Yaana turns even redder, her head visibly spinning.

I know she's not, but she looks drunk herself.

"I won't say such things!"

"But you said it was sacred, right? Come on—you're a holy woman. Can't you educate poor, ignorant me?"

"Wehhh! Weeeehhh!"

I know it's half Yaana's own fault, but I still feel bad for her.

I'd better cut this short.

"Hyrince, that's enough teasing for now."

"Heh-heh. I guess so. Now that I know Yaana's actually a perv, that's good enough for me."

"A p-p-p-p-pervert? Me?!"

"Well, you're clearly obsessed with the subject, yeah? Otherwise you wouldn't be overreacting like this."

"Who's obsessed?!"

"Now, now. It's nothing unusual for youngsters our age to start taking an interest in that sort of thing. Besides, you said it yourself—it's 'sacred' and 'noble.' So as a saint who serves the gods, you could even say it's your duty to take an interest."

"M-my duty?"

"Yeah, exactly. So there's nothing to be ashamed of. Just be honest with yourself."

"Honest with myself..."

"To start with, try thinking about the person you like and all your feelings for them!"

"......"

Yaana turns toward me with an oddly feverish gaze.

"Yaana. *Yaana.* He's messing with you again."

"Wha—?!"

Coming back to her senses, Yaana glares at Hyrince and sees that he's clutching his stomach and shaking with the effort of holding in his laughter.

"HYYYYRIIIIIINCE?!"

"Ha-ha-ha! Sorry, sorry." Hyrince chokes out an apology through his laughter. "But it really isn't such a bad thing to be honest with yourself, you know? We're at the age where it's perfectly normal to have those kinds of thoughts. Even Julius is a growing boy, too, no matter how noble and innocent he might act."

"Hyrince…"

Now it's my turn to glare at Hyrince, but he shrugs, looking unfazed.

"In fact, sometimes it's the straitlaced types who end up falling for someone with major sex appeal, 'cause they've been suppressing their urges for so long. The more you suppress something, the bigger it'll blow up when the time comes. If you keep dawdling, someone might come along and steal him away."

"Wha—?!" Yaana shrieks.

"Like that other apprentice Aurel. She's pretty close with Julius, y'know? And her face is plain, but she's been growing like crazy lately."

Hyrince glances pointedly at Yaana's chest and snorts.

Of course, that sends Yaana flying into another fit of rage.

Yaana's not, you know…small, either.

I think she's very pretty, with a well-balanced figure.

It's just that Aurel is, um, very blessed in that department.

I still have a strange bond with Aurel, since she's my master's second apprentice.

We first met in the former Keren County.

After that, she showed magical promise and insisted on becoming his second apprentice, so we spent a lot of time together for a while.

I still see her pretty regularly.

And every time we meet again, she's, um…grown.

Her chest, I mean.

"Hmph! Julius wouldn't be seduced by those pointlessly giant sacks of fat! Right, Julius?!"

She looks to me a little desperately, but honestly, I'm not quite sure how to answer.

Unable to confirm or deny right away, all I can do is smile vaguely.

Somehow, this only makes Yaana look even more shocked.

"You two adults! Stop pretending not to hear us and say something!"

Yaana's glare swivels toward Jeskan and Hawkin.

"I'm not sure what to tell you, missy. I've messed around a fair amount, so I don't think I can give you the answer you want."

"H-how indecent!"

Yaana huffs at Jeskan.

"Now, I do think it's normal to be sensitive about this topic at your age, but personally, I think it's better if Julius gets a little bit of experience in that department," he continues.

"Don't try to tempt Julius down the path of evil!"

Turning bright red, Yaana flails her hands around.

All the fruit juice seems to have splashed out of her cup at this point.

"I'm serious, Miss Yaana. Many a great man has fallen to feminine wiles before. He has to build up some resistance to that kind of sexuality, or he really could get hoodwinked, like Hyrince says. In Julius's position, he could be in danger of someone seducing him to keep him from interfering with an evil plot or even to try and assassinate him."

Yaana shrinks back in response to the unexpectedly serious topic, probably embarrassed about getting so worked up.

"S'normal for a lass your age to be prim 'n' proper, li'l Yaana. But I wanna make sure ya know, there are some real nice ladies who happen to make their livin' in just that sort of business. It ain't right to dismiss every one of 'em as evil, y'know?"

"Right."

Hawkin, who's knowledgeable about all kinds of trades and secrets, makes a surprisingly earnest comment as well, and Yaana nods obediently.

She's probably remembering that there are many women who enter the nighttime entertainment business because of poverty or other circumstances.

"I ain't sayin' Julius should mess around with women for fun, o'course. Although I'd say it might not be a bad thing to get some experience at a trustworthy establishment. But there might be other ways to learn that kind of thing for royalty, so maybe I'm worryin' for nothing. And if ya got your little heart set on someone already, that's all right, too."

Yaana looks at me with obvious hope in her eyes, but I manage to pretend not to notice.

"I hear there's a race of demons who specialize in seduction, too. The demons are quiet of late, but if the war starts again, Julius will have to go to the front lines, being the hero and all. And then he might have to deal with that sort of thing."

The war against demons.

Usually, it's the biggest duty assigned to the hero.

They say that generations of heroes have dedicated most of their lives to this cause.

But in the era of the previous hero, the demons suddenly stopped their usual onslaught of attacks on humanity and became almost disturbingly quiet.

That uneasy peace continues to this day, so I haven't had to fight any demons yet.

But if they ever start attacking humanity again, it'll be my duty as the hero to stave them off.

If that day comes, I'm sure it'll be a fearsome battle.

A cloud falls over the faces of the others, who must be thinking about the same thing.

"Don't worry. I wouldn't fall for a trap that easily. If anything, I'd be more afraid of Hyrince getting charmed straight to his doom."

"Hey, it wouldn't be so bad to die at the hands of a pretty lady!"

Hyrince immediately matches my joke with one of his own.

"Honestly! Hyrince, you're far more worrisome than Julius!"

Yaana promptly starts scolding him, and Jeskan and Hawkin chuckle.

I can't help wishing that times like these would go on forever.

Sophia's Diary 8

Bones!

Hmm? Today's bones are especially crunchy.

Wait, these are dragon bones?

Well, no wonder, then.

I feel like Goody Two-shoes has been all over me even more so than usual lately.

He keeps touching me whenever he gets the chance, you know?

Unlike the other brats, at least he isn't trying anything stupid like flipping my skirt, but I guess he's a boy, too.

That's just the sort of thing a boy his age would do.

Hmm?

Where is he trying to touch me, you ask?

Mostly on the head and the face.

He's even smelled my hair and other weirdness like that.

And I guess he's also tried to touch my butt and chest and stuff.

Huh? What? Don't ever let him touch me again?

It's dangerous?

Men are animals?

Where did you learn a phrase like—? No, never mind. I know the answer to that.

But he's still just a little boy, you know.

Certainly not old enough to be called a man yet.

What's that?

Men are dangerous no matter what the age?

Look, isn't that a little bit paranoid?

All right, all right!

I won't let him touch me again.

Not even my hair?

Of course not.

Huh?

Be careful with my belongings?

Don't play the recorder?

??? Why would I have a recorder?

What in the world are you talking about?

J9 Julius, Age 15: Partner

The strangely beautiful sight almost takes my breath away.

If it wasn't the very incarnation of disaster, I might have even wanted to keep watching it forever.

I gaze up at the enormous, shimmering scarlet bird flying above us.

Each flap of its wings produces a dazzling flame from its wing tips, creating a wondrous trail of light behind it.

The legendary-class monster, the phoenix.

As the name implies, it's a monster that is thought to be immortal.

It's said that when someone succeeded in Appraising it long ago, it was found to have the Immortality skill. There are many people who doubt that legend, but no one has ever succeeded in bringing down the phoenix.

The creature usually dwells on a volcano and doesn't attack people.

Thus, it's not generally considered a threat to humanity, so any adventurers who challenge it seeking fame or rare materials do so at their own risk.

Most people who go after it never return, proving that it deserves its rank as legendary.

Legendary-class monsters are so dangerous that they're assumed untouchable by humans.

If one of them happens to turn their fangs on humans, we'd be destroyed without any way of fighting back.

Just like the Nightmare of the Labyrinth...

But the phoenix has never attacked us, with one sole exception, so it's not usually considered much of a threat.

Unfortunately, that one exception is happening right now.

A huge crowd of humans runs after the flying bird, myself included.

It's the phoenix's migration season.

Once every few decades, the creature moves to a new nest.

Its destination depends purely on the phoenix's whims.

Sometimes it will settle down right near its previous nest, while other times, it's been known to wander for months.

Some records even say that it's moved between continents.

The sight of the phoenix soaring through the sky in search of a new nest is truly fantastical and beautiful.

But this is a legendary-class monster.

Just by flying, it causes catastrophic damage to the area around it.

The swirling flames created by each flap of its wings burn the ground.

It leaves nothing but scorched earth behind it, devoid of a single blade of grass.

This isn't such a problem if it's flying at a high elevation, but sometimes it flies low to the ground on a whim.

If there should happen to be a human settlement below it, then disaster would be unavoidable.

Thus, whenever the phoenix migrates, it's customary for people to follow behind it and keep watch like this.

And in a way, it's sort of like a festival, too.

"A feather!"

"It's mine! I called this one!"

One of the phoenix's feathers flutters down from the sky.

Many in the group following the bird surge forward.

The feather of the phoenix is an incredibly valuable item.

It has the extraordinary one-use-only ability to protect the holder from death.

Even if the person who possesses it is mortally wounded, it's said that the feather can instantly restore them to health, though only once.

For people like adventurers and knights, who are constantly at risk of death, it's a highly sought-after item.

But it comes from a legendary-class monster, so it's not very easy to come by.

Though it's an item that helps the user avoid death, one would have to risk death to get it in the first place.

Still, there's a dubious legend that eating the phoenix's heart would grant one eternal life, and selling a single feather fetches an exorbitant price, so that doesn't stop overly ambitious adventurers from attempting to bring it down.

The main takeaway is that during this rare migration, acquiring those valuable feathers can be done relatively safely.

Thus, people come from all over to follow the migration in the hopes of acquiring a feather.

Still, it's not an easy job. The phoenix isn't particularly fast for a legendary-class monster, but it's still difficult to keep up without a horse or something like that.

Indeed, most of us are currently riding mounts that excel in endurance.

But even then, if it crosses through areas like mountains or forests where horses can't easily pass, the only way to continue is on foot.

Terrain doesn't matter to the phoenix, since it's flying in the air.

Still, we have little choice but to chase this creature indefinitely, until it settles on its next nest.

And if its path leads toward a human settlement, we have to run ahead of it and evacuate the area.

It's not just humans who are affected, either.

At times, the phoenix's path might cross the habitats of other monsters. If it destroys their nests, they sometimes become displaced and change the surrounding ecosystem.

They could even affect nearby towns and villages when they relocate.

Part of our job as we follow the phoenix is to mitigate damage like that by predicting the phoenix's route and reporting to the adventurers' guild.

"They're awfully energetic."

Hyrince sounds a little tired as he watches the group scrambling for the feather.

"Well, that's why most of them are here."

"Yeah, but it's been ten days now..."

Hyrince groans in exhaustion, and I answer with a dry smile.

That's right: We've already been following the phoenix for ten days.

The legendary monster can fly indefinitely during its migration, and we have to follow it for as long as it takes.

Since that leaves little time for sleeping and eating, a staggering exhaustion has overtaken most of us.

"Dammit. Must be nice to get some rest."

Hyrince glowers at Yaana, who's sound asleep—in my arms.

We're currently riding a horse together so I can hold up Yaana while she sleeps.

This is the only way anyone can get any rest.

We have to eat handheld foods while riding on our horse, too.

The biggest inconvenience is when someone has to do their business, in which case the only choice is to stop the horse, dismount, take care of it quickly, then catch up to the rest of the group.

Of course, there aren't any toilets or anything, so you have to do it right out in the open.

As a result, Yaana is the only female in the group.

This grueling march would be especially tough on a woman in many ways, so it's understandable.

I suggested before we left that maybe Yaana should sit this one out, but she refused, insisting that it's the duty of the saint to be at the hero's side at all times.

As I expected, she's already run out of strength partway through. I can't blame her, since even Hyrince is becoming both physically and mentally exhausted.

"Yaana should really be more cautious anyway. A girl her age shouldn't be jumping in with a big band of men like this."

"I'm sure that's just how much she trusts Julius. He'd never do anything to her, and he wouldn't let anyone else take advantage of her, either."

Jeskan tries to smooth things over, but Hyrince is being grouchier than usual.

"Well, I think she's too dependent on him. It's the saint's job to support the hero, but Julius is literally supporting her instead."

"You say that, but you're really worried about her, right?"

I wish he would just admit that he's worried that she might be in danger.

Hyrince is always so contrary.

"Y'know, I've been wondering," Jeskan says bluntly. "Are you in love with Yaana, Hyrince?"

"'Scuse me?"

To be honest, I've been wondering the same thing.

Hyrince is always hiding his emotions, so it's occurred to me that maybe he teases and insults Yaana so much because he's actually interested in her.

But Yaana very obviously has feelings for me.

So I've been worried for a while that Hyrince is holding off and keeping his distance out of consideration for that. I couldn't bring myself to ask, but I worried that he was suppressing his feelings for Yaana because of me—but he promptly denies it.

"Yeah, no, not a chance. I swear to the gods, I'm definitely not in love with that one."

"Wait, really?"

"Yeah. To be honest, there's a different girl I like."

This is news to me.

I've never seen him show feelings toward anyone before, so I assumed he might be interested in Yaana, since she's so close to us.

"Who is it?"

Jeskan grins as he presses Hyrince further.

Some say that women love to talk about romance, but the truth is that men love it just as much.

I'm very interested to know who this apparent childhood love of Hyrince's is, too.

"It's a secret."

"C'mon, you can tell us. Please? It must be a childhood friend, right?"

I join in with Jeskan on interrogating Hyrince.

"I'm not telling... We can't be together anyway."

When I see Hyrince's expression, I regret asking him so lightly.

We've known each other for a long time, but I've never seen him make a face like this before.

His expression is a complex mixture of love, sorrow, and regret.

As soon as I see it, I get the sense that this person is someone he can never meet again.

Maybe she only exists in his memories now.

"Sorry."

"Forgive us."

"It's fine."

Jeskan and I apologize, but Hyrince smiles gently as if in forgiveness.

In that moment, though not for the first time, Hyrince seems mature beyond his years.

"Forget about me, though. What about you, Julius? You gonna respond to Yaana's feelings or what?"

Hyrince changes the subject by turning it toward me, and Jeskan jumps on board.

"Good point. Little Miss Yaana's interest is pretty obvious, eh?"

I don't really want to talk about this, but we just forced a painful confession out of Hyrince, so it wouldn't be fair for me to refuse to answer.

"I'm planning on being single for my entire life."

In other words…I don't intend to respond to Yaana's feelings.

"And why is that?"

At Jeskan's question, I take a moment to close my eyes and get my thoughts in order.

"I doubt I'm going to live a long life," I say at last, opening my eyes. "My master once told me that if you can't discern between what you can and can't do, you'll just hasten your death. So I'm sure I'll die while trying to achieve my reckless goals."

I've been thinking about this for a long time.

My goal is a peaceful world where everyone can live with smiles on their faces.

But I'm fully aware that it's realistically impossible.

My strength can only go so far.

Hero or not, I can't even beat Master in a fight, and I'm sure I couldn't defeat this flying legendary-class monster, either.

There's so little I can actually do.

But I've decided to keep moving forward toward my ideals anyway.

I want to keep aiming for that goal, even though I know it's impossible.

It's the very recklessness that Master warned me against.

So I'm bound to die sooner rather than later.

"Master said that there's no point living the way you wish if you don't live long…but I can't give up on chasing my ideals, even if it means running up against obstacles I'm not strong enough to overcome. I'll keep fighting until I truly can't take another step."

But I don't intend to bring anyone else down with me.

"I do want Yaana to be happy. So I can't take her hand knowing that I'm going to die young."

Hyrince heaves a sigh at my answer, while Jeskan nods quietly.

"If that's the answer you've chosen, I won't try to meddle with it," says Jeskan.

But Hyrince seems to object.

"Well, if you ask me, you should grab her hand anyway. It's not like you dislike her, right? In fact, you love her, don't you?"

"…I guess so. But I think that's exactly why it has to be this way."

I want her to be happy because I love her, I think.

"Then why don't you just be with her already?"

"If only it were that easy."

"Okay, look. If you die, Yaana's gonna be sad either way. Your death will weigh her down for the rest of her life."

"But she'll still have the possibility of a happy future with someone else. I can't let her whole life go to waste just because of my short-lived feelings."

"Why would being close with you mean her life goes to waste? She's gonna be miserable when you die either way, but at least you could leave her some happy memories if you're together in the meantime, right?"

Hyrince's words remind me of what my master said to me and how Mr. Tiva lived.

"Besides, I've got a bone to pick with the assumption that you're gonna die young in the first place."

Hyrince glares at me but then heaves an exaggerated sigh.

"Ugh… I can't believe the hero of all people has a death wish. Talk about a letdown. I'm sooo disappointed."

"What's that supposed to mean?"

"You really think a coward who's already resigned himself to dying can accomplish anything? You can fight like your life's on the line and get into life-and-death battles, but you still gotta try to live."

At first, I can't tell if Hyrince is joking around or not.

But I think he must be expressing his true feelings.

"Yeah. You're right. It's not like I intend to die."

"That's the spirit. If you die, it'll be after I go down first. 'Cause I'm always gonna protect the lot of you."

"I'm sure you will."

"Ah, to be young again," Jeskan murmurs with a smile as he observes our exchange.

Just then—Hawkin, who was running ahead, speeds back toward us on his horse.

"Bad news. There's a village coming up!"

"All right. Everyone! Did you hear that?! We have to get in front of the phoenix and evacuate the people from the village!"

When I shout orders at the group, they respond with a chorus of affirmations.

"Yaana, wake up."

"Mm...nnngh."

Yaana groans in her sleep in a strangely sexy way.

I'm probably overthinking it because of the conversation we just had.

"Yaana...," I prompt her a little more loudly.

"Ah! The Eyeball King!"

Yaana sits up with a start, shouting nonsensically.

What kind of dream was she having?

"Huh? The Eyeball King found out about the Ear Queen's affair with the Lip Knight? Wha—?"

Seriously, what was that dream about?!

I'm a little intrigued, but now isn't the time.

As soon as Yaana wakes up completely, we hurry to pass the flying immortal and reach the village first.

"What? You want us to evacuate?! What will happen to our homes?!"

Once we explain to the villagers that the phoenix is coming, and we shout at them to evacuate, one of the men starts complaining.

This isn't our first time calling for an evacuation in a settlement, and we've encountered similar reactions before.

Usually, repeating the explanation a few times gets them to give in, but this time is different.

"If my house burns down, I won't be able to live anymore, dammit! I'mma stay here and protect my house!"

The man refuses to listen or budge an inch.

"Mister, staying here'll only put you in danger. How're you gonna protect your house? You'll just go up in flames along with it!"

"The hell if I care! This house is my whole life! If it burns down, there ain't no point in me survivin' anyway!"

Even Hyrince can't persuade him.

"Sir Hero, what should we do?" one of the members of the troop asks.

I'm at a loss, too.

"Wait, you're the hero?"

The man turns to me.

"Yes, that's right."

Hoping this might give me a chance to convince him, I decide to try talking to him.

"If you're the hero, then protect my house! You can do that much, can't you?!"

"Well…"

"Listen, Mister. Give it up already. If we could do that, we wouldn't be evacuating you, would we?"

"Why the hell not?! You're the hero, aren't you?! Then you oughta save me! Right?!"

The man clings to the walls of his house and breaks down in tears.

He must have a deep attachment to the house. At this rate, he really will go down in flames with it.

"…All right."

"Oi!" Hyrince grabs my shoulder.

The rest of the group stirs up in alarm, too.

"Really?!"

"Yes. I'll take responsibility for protecting this house. So in exchange, please evacuate somewhere safe."

"You ain't just gonna abandon it once I leave?"

"No. I promise."

I look the man straight in the eye.

"Thank you."

Apparently believing my words, the man lets go of his house, grabs my hand, and bows his head deeply.

Then he joins the rest of the villagers in evacuating, led by our group.

"Well? What're you going to do now?"

"I don't know. What should I do?"

"You didn't even have a plan, huh…?" Hyrince shakes his head and groans. "I don't suppose you'd be willing to give up on it?"

"I promised I wouldn't."

Hyrince heaves a long sigh, then looks at the rest of our party as if for help.

"If Julius says he's going to protect it, then it's my job as the saint to support him!"

"We've got no choice but to do it at this point, I suppose."

"Pshhh. S'not like we gotta beat that thing, right? There has to be a way to keep the house intact, I reckon."

Hyrince's shoulders slump at their responses.

"You'll protect us, right?" I prod him jokingly.

"Aaargh! Fine, fine!" Hyrince sighs again and gives in, then looks to Hawkin. "So how exactly are we gonna do this?"

"The phoenix's a legendary-class monster, y'know? No sense fighting it when we wouldn't stand a chance in hell."

Hawkin is the most knowledgeable of anyone in our group.

And it's always been his job to come up with strategies for us based on that knowledge.

"So we just gotta get it to go around this village without fightin' it, eh?"

And so we set about putting Hawkin's plan into action.

Smoke rises ahead on the phoenix's flight path.

The monster changes directions to go around it, as if repulsed by the smoke.

How did we do it? It's simple.

We created a bonfire that produces smoke with a scent that repels the phoenix and used Wind Magic to control it.

Thus, we guided the monster into changing its course to avoid the smoke.

The phoenix shows itself to people relatively easily compared with other legendary-class monsters, so there is a fair amount of research on it.

In other words, there is information about what the phoenix avoids, and we were able to use it to drive the phoenix away.

However, there is a downside to this method. The source of the smell that the phoenix dislikes so much is a very valuable material.

Namely: fire dragon dung.

The phoenix is a fire monster, too, but apparently, they get along very poorly, so it will never make its nest in a place where fire dragons dwell.

That's why we burned fire dragon dung to produce the scent of fire dragons, causing the phoenix to avoid it.

But the fire dragon is at minimum an S-rank monster.

Some particularly strong fire dragons have even been deemed legendary-class, the same as the phoenix itself.

On top of that, fire dragons usually travel in flocks and live in treacherous areas like active volcanos.

Harvesting their dung is at least as dangerous as collecting a phoenix feather, maybe even more so.

This valuable dung is used when the phoenix travels toward a large population center. If there's too many people to evacuate quickly, it's safer to change the phoenix's course instead.

It's common knowledge that large towns often keep fire dragon dung on hand in case of such an emergency.

That's where we were able to borrow a very small amount of that dragon dung, which we burned to produce this smoke.

Normally, it's the kind of valuable material that should be preserved, but using a tiny amount of it like this isn't enough to be a problem.

Of course, this tiny amount alone wouldn't produce enough smoke to ward off the phoenix, so we used Wind Magic to gather it all up and focus it close to the phoenix's nose.

"I guess I'd expect no less of the number one apprentice of the world's strongest mage."

Jeskan sounds impressed.

Unfortunately, I can't even respond to him right now.

Magic spells normally have a set form and amount of power.

Master is the first person in the world to change that.

Instead of simply "producing" magic, you have to "control" it.

Considering that no one else in history had ever accomplished such a feat, it's obviously not easy.

Normally, the most a Wind Magic spell can do is push wind in a particular direction.

Using it to collect smoke, and then carry it to the phoenix's nose, is incredibly difficult.

If I lose focus for even a second, the spell will collapse, and the smoke will likely disperse.

It's not a flashy spell by any means, yet in a way, it's more difficult than even invoking massive magic.

"Great! The phoenix is changing its course. A little more to the right."

Following Hyrince's instructions, I manipulate the smoke to guide the phoenix farther from us.

At this rate, we should be able to keep it away entirely.

But just as I think we've succeeded, the wind suddenly blows.

"Ah?!"

It's not magic—just a natural gust of wind.

But it pushes the smoke right into the phoenix's face.

"SKREEEEE!"

The phoenix lets out a high-pitched shriek.

"Oh no!"

The phoenix doesn't attack humans unprovoked and is said to have a gentler temperament than most legendary-class monsters.

But still, you can't let your guard down around it.

Using smoke to guide it away wasn't enough to provoke it to attack us, but it looks like throwing the smoke right into its face is another story.

The phoenix is coming this way—with obvious anger in its eyes.

"Jeskan! Take Yaana and Hawkin and run!" I shout immediately.

Jeskan obeys at once, scooping up Yaana and Hawkin under his arms and sprinting away.

"Wait! No!"

Yaana tries to resist, but Jeskan doesn't slow down.

He knows perfectly well what happens if you try to fight a legendary-class monster.

The phoenix spreads its wings, and I run out in front of it.

I have to buy time for the others to get away.

It's me the monster is after.

I dragged the others into this stupid plan, so I have to make sure I'm the only one who suffers the consequences!

The phoenix flaps its wings, sending a whirl of flames toward me.

I produce my Light Magic barrier.

But even with as much magic power as I could put into it, it burns away like paper.

"Shield!"

In the last moment before my barrier dissipates completely, Hyrince jumps in front of me with his shield at the ready.

"Hyrince!"

My shout is drowned out by the roar of flames.

The attack lasts only a second.

But in that second, I can clearly see the flames burning through Hyrince's shield and searing his body.

Since Hyrince protected me, I suffered only light burns from the attack.

The flames whirl away, and my vision clears.

Before my eyes, I see Hyrince—his entire body covered in burns yet still standing with his shield raised.

The single attack seems to have satisfied the phoenix; it gives us one last look, then flaps away.

A moment later, Hyrince slumps over and falls to the ground.

"Hyrince!"

I sprint up to my fallen friend, quickly beating away the flames still licking his body.

"Hyrince?!" I hear Yaana cry out behind me.

Jeskan is running back toward us with her over his shoulder.

"Yaana! Please heal him!"

"Right away!"

Yaana uses Healing Magic.

I follow suit, trying to soothe the wounds that cover Hyrince's body.

"Hyrince! Don't you die on me!"

I keep using Healing Magic with every last ounce of my strength.

Hawkin produces a vial from his pocket and pours the liquid over Hyrince: a healing potion.

"Nnngh!"

"Hyrince!"

Finally, Hyrince coughs and groans.

"...I'm not gonna die. 'Cause if I do, it'd be your turn next, right?"

His voice is faint but steady.

"That was so reckless..."

"You're one to talk."

Hyrince narrowly escaped death.

As if to reward his efforts, a single phoenix feather flutters down from the sky, landing right next to him.

Although Hyrince survived, we determined that we couldn't keep following the phoenix any longer, so we decided to leave it to the others to take care of things.

When they saw Hyrince's condition, the villagers allowed us to stay the night.

We laid Hyrince down to get some rest in the room they gave us.

Before long, the man who'd prompted us to stay and deal with the phoenix by refusing to evacuate unless we protected his house comes to check on us.

When he sees Hyrince's battered state, his face turns pale.

"I-is this...because of me?"

"...Your house is safe, just like we promised."

"I...I—I built that house with my wife, who passed away, so..."

"Well, we protected it," Hyrince grunts curtly.

"...Thank you so much!"

The man bows his head and hurries out of the room.

"See? This is what we get for putting our lives on the line for selfish people like that guy. Are you satisfied, Julius?"

Hyrince looks at me seriously.

I'm sure he's trying to tell me that I should stop blindly offering to help anyone and everyone I meet.

And in a way, he's saying that this is my fault, too.

We agreed to that man's request because of my own selfish insistence.

If we'd dragged him away from the house and made him evacuate by force, we wouldn't have been put in such danger, and Hyrince wouldn't have nearly died.

So Hyrince is right to be angry.

I think he's especially angry with me for being reckless, too.

And yet...even so, if I was put in the same situation again, I think I would make the same choice.

"I'm sorry, Hyrince. But I still want to keep reaching out my hand to people in need. I feel bad for making you go along with my selfishness, though."

"Selfishness, huh? Listen. I don't think you can call that selfishness. It's people like that guy who are selfish. I'd call you softhearted, that's what."

Hyrince sighs irritably.

"He was selfish, I know. But he did thank us, and he seemed to feel guilty that you got hurt. I think this incident must have made him realize how selfish he was. So I think the gratitude he feels toward us today will be passed on in the form of kindness to someone else tomorrow. I really do believe that."

"...Seriously, how soft can you get?"

Hyrince closes his eyes, as if to say he's given up.

"Hyrince, I'm sorry."

"...It's fine. I knew what I was getting into." He smiles wanly. "But I just want to say that people aren't as good as you want them to be. For all we know, helping that guy today might just make him assume that he'll always get help whenever he wants it. There are people who are grateful when you save them, and some of them might try to learn from your example and pay it forward. But that's not gonna apply to everyone. At least remember that much."

"...Okay."

I'm sure Hyrince is right.

Some people won't change, no matter how hard I try.

Just like the criminals from the human-trafficking organization.

And there are probably people who will consider my help convenient and nothing more.

As sad as it is, I don't have the power to change everyone's hearts.

I softly touch my scarf.

My sadness must be evident in my expression, because Hyrince offers me some comfort.

"Don't make that face. I'm following you because I like that soft side of yours. And that's never gonna change."

His words are an indirect promise that he'll always stay by my side.

To be honest, part of me feared that after making him do something so reckless, Hyrince wouldn't want to follow me anymore.

So I'm thrilled, and relieved, to know that he's going to stay with me.

"You being reckless isn't anything new, right? These injuries just prove that I couldn't keep up with your craziness."

"That's not true."

The phoenix's flames might have easily killed even me if they'd hit me directly.

The only reason I'm practically unharmed is because Hyrince covered me with his own body.

If anything, I'm the one who couldn't keep up with Hyrince, since he had to protect me.

"Hyrince, I really am sorry. And thank you."

"Sure."

I'm sorry for making you do something so crazy.

And thank you for staying by my side anyway.

"Oh, I know. Here."

I hold out to Hyrince the phoenix feather I picked up.

"What's this?"

"You should carry it."

Hyrince doesn't seem to understand why I'm offering him the feather.

"Huh? Why should I be the one to take it? You hold on to it."

Hyrince tries to push it away, but I force it into his hand and close his fingers around it.

"Hey!"

"You keep it, Hyrince."

"Seriously, why?! Do you even understand how important you are?! It's way more important that you stay alive than me! You should be the one to take it!"

Hyrince tries to shove it back to me, but I refuse to take it.

"Don't worry. I won't die."

"What are you talking about?!"

"You said so yourself, right? If I die, it'll be after you do."

When I use his own words against him, Hyrince is stunned into silence.

He's the one who swore that he would protect me as long as he's alive, after all.

"I'm not going to die. Since you're our shield user, your chances of dying are much higher, right? So it's better if you take it, Hyrince."

"You're unbelievable…" Still lying down, Hyrince clutches his forehead and groans. "But that's got nothing to do with this. You take the damn thing already."

"No! I! Won't!"

"You damn idiot!"

We continue to argue back and forth until Hyrince finally passes out from exhaustion.

You know, Hyrince…

Like I said about Yaana, I want you to be happy, too.

HYRINCE QUARTO

The second son of Duke Quarto of the Analeit Kingdom. His much older brother is already in line to be the heir of the dukedom and even has a son of his own who is naturally favored to be the next heir, so Hyrince's standing is quite uncertain. He and Julius are childhood friends, being in similarly strange positions. Due to their bond, he becomes Julius's attendant and supports him both publicly and privately. He has the air of a jokester and frequently teases Yaana, but he's actually very thoughtful and cares deeply for his friends. As the shield bearer of the party, he has a desire to protect his friends that manifests in his instinct to throw himself between them and any amount of danger.

Sophia's Diary 9

Mm. The bones are pretty tasty today.

Huh? Do I have a fever or something?

Hmm, I guess you're not wrong about that, exactly.

I've been feeling sort of off lately, you see.

Feverish, you might even say.

Ah, but I don't actually have a fever.

It's just that my body feels heavy, and I'm kind of listless.

Other symptoms?

Oh, well, I guess I've been getting urges lately when I look at boys' necks.

Do I *vant to suck their blood?*

Where did you learn that—? No, never mind, I already know the answer.

But yes, I suppose I do have a craving for some blood.

Don't worry, though—I won't.

These brats are super annoying, but obviously I'm not going to attack them.

I'll manage, trust me.

J10 Julius, Age 16: Friends

"Heya. Been a while."

Two swaying mounds.

Even through her clothes, the movement is obvious.

Watching me like a hawk, Yaana notices my gaze and nudges me sharply with an elbow.

"Hi, Aurel. It's been a while."

I compose myself and greet my fellow apprentice.

Right now, we're in a certain town in the empire.

"All they told us was to meet with the person in charge here, but I had no idea it was you, Aurel."

"Ah-ha-ha, right? I am a mage of the imperial court, y'see, believe it or not. Heh. Y'never know what the hell's gonna happen in life, huh?"

Aurel grins, looking nostalgic.

She was originally Master's caretaker, but he determined that she had magical potential and made her his second apprentice. Apparently, this led to her becoming a court mage.

Aurel herself had only ever planned on getting a random job, getting randomly married, and living a somewhat random life, but things have turned out very different for her.

"Is it tough work, being a court mage?"

"Damn right it is." She gives me a dead-eyed look. "All the other mages are just as pervy as our dumbass master, y'know. And they call me 'ma'am,' too! They're way older than I am, dammit!"

A group of old men like our master?

Yeah, that definitely sounds tough to deal with.

"Oh, but enough about my gripes. Let's talk business. The guild master's waiting for us, so c'mon with me, please."

With that, Aurel leads us toward the adventurers' guild.

"Seems like we're kinda linked to this guild by fate, huh?"

"What do you mean?" I ask.

"You know, the mutated ogre that got away from Master?"

"Ahhh, I see. That was here?"

I've heard about this before: the unique ogre that appeared in the empire.

It was far more powerful than any individual ogre should be, and it brought down many adventurers before our master was sent out to deal with it.

Master even went into battle against it with the world's strongest swordsman, yet it still escaped from both of them, which became major news.

However, the ogre hasn't been seen since it ran off into the Mystic Mountains, so it's assumed that it was killed by the ice dragons that live there.

And apparently, this is the very town where that ogre first appeared.

"Ugh. Collecting herbs again?"

"Don't complain, Kunihiko."

As we arrive at the adventurers' guild, two kids around Shun's age are leaving the building. The boy's eyes briefly meet mine as we pass each other.

"Hey, if it ain't Mr. Gotou. Is the guild master around?"

"Oh, hey there, Aurel. Just a second."

The man walks into the back of the guild hall with practiced steps.

That part of the guild is off-limits to anyone but employees, and this Mr. Gotou looks more like an adventurer to me. Is he allowed back there?

"Come on through, he says."

"Gotcha. All right, this way."

Once Gotou calls out from farther inside, Aurel heads in, motioning for us to follow.

Down the hall, we reach the guild master's office and enter. Awaiting us inside are Mr. Gotou and an older man who's probably the guild master.

"We deeply appreciate you coming, Sir Hero," says the man. "I am the guild master here."

"And I'm Gotou, an adventurer in these parts. It's an honor to meet you."

"My name is Julius Zagan Analeit, the hero."

Once our introductions are complete, the guild master gestures for us to take a seat.

"Well then, let's get right to it, if you don't mind. How much have you heard so far, Sir Hero?"

"Very little."

We haven't been given any real details about why we're here, just that an unexpectedly troublesome situation has arisen.

"I see. Well, I suppose I'll explain from the beginning, then."

With that, the guild master starts explaining the trouble in the town, or rather in its immediate vicinity.

"This town is very close to the Mystic Mountains. And if you go a bit farther east, you'll reach the buffer zone with the demon-realm border. In short, the demon realm is quite close by."

This town is at the very border of the empire, so it's a hairbreadth away from the demons.

"However, it's impossible to cross the Mystic Mountains. It isn't as if there are no routes around the range at all, but there are tribes that guard those areas. It might not be quite as dangerous as the open mountains, but it's still very harsh. In other words, demons almost never make their way through to here."

On top of being inhabited by ice dragons, the Mystic Mountains are far too cold for anyone to regularly traverse.

The only paths around the mountains are inhabited by clans that make their living hunting demons.

So while it might be close to the demon realm, there's little fear of demons invading here.

"But there was an incident a few years ago where one of those clans was slaughtered by one of the Demon Lord's subordinates. And therein lies the problem."

"Are you saying demons have started attacking?"

"Not exactly. Well, demons have come through, but not to attack us."

I assumed this meant that the demons were taking this chance to slowly advance, but it appears I was wrong. But he's saying a demon did come?

"What is it, then?"

"Demon refugees."

That was the last thing I expected to hear.

"What? Refugees?"

Sitting next to me, Yaana widens her eyes in confusion.

Incidentally, Aurel is sitting on my other side.

And the sofa isn't particularly large, so we're all packed pretty close together.

I know this isn't the time to worry about such things, but the soft feelings on either side of me are very…distracting.

No! This is serious. I have to focus.

"There are very few of them who have made it through, but since that clan was destroyed, the occasional demon has attempted to use that gap to reach us here. And they all invariably say they're fleeing the demon realm. In short, they've come here because they can't live there any longer."

For a moment, I'm stunned into silence by his explanation.

Demons are the fated enemy of humanity.

They're a symbol of terror and our constant opponent in an endless war.

So who would expect some of those demons to flee their territory and come to the land of humans as refugees?

"Erm, so…where are they now?"

"While I do pity them, we certainly can't let demons enter the human realm, so we either send them back or dispose of them here."

So they try to run away only to be met by a cruel fate?

I can't help feeling bad for them, even if they are demons.

"We've interrogated captured demons about the situation in the demon realm, and it appears things are quite bad over there."

"How do you mean?"

"It seems that ever since a new Demon Lord took over, the taxes, forced enlistment, and so on have all been quite harsh."

I'd already heard through the Word of God religion that there was a new Demon Lord in charge.

I didn't know what sort of person that was, of course, but it sounds like they must be a terrible tyrant.

"So that's why they're fleeing? Guess demons don't have it easy, either," Hyrince murmurs.

"But that's all just the setup. This is where the real problem begins."

The guild master produces a single piece of paper.

"What's that?"

"One of the demon men who made it here was carrying this. He said he came to deliver it to us."

"May I take a look?"

"It's written in the demon language..."

"That's all right. I can read it."

I've studied demon language thoroughly in preparation for a possible war, so I can converse and read in it without a problem.

And the paper now in my hands contains startling revelations.

To summarize: The new Demon Lord's rule is so severe that they're plotting an uprising.

They want to cooperate with humans to defeat the Demon Lord.

This Demon Lord is incredibly powerful, so they hope to borrow the strength of the hero for this.

And they want to meet in secret to discuss this possible deal.

"It's suspicious."

"Very suspicious."

"Smells like a trap, all right."

Hyrince, Jeskan, and Hawkin immediately suspect a trap.

"But it's true that the demon realm is in such a terrible state that many demons are trying to flee into our lands, right?" says Yaana. "So maybe they really are asking for our help?"

The letter contains a time and place for the secret meeting.

It's set to happen in a deep forest in the buffer zone with the demon realm.

And the appointed time is just a few days from now.

"It definitely sounds like a trap to me," Hyrince grumbles.

"I know." I nod.

"Then why are we walking straight into that trap, huh?"

"I guess we're betting on the tiny chance that it isn't actually a trap."

We're currently in the forest, heading toward the meeting point specified in the letter.

As far as the authenticity of the letter, we reached the conclusion that it's almost certainly a trap.

It's true that demon refugees have been filtering over the border, but it's still absurd to think that they would turn to their bitter rivals, the humans, to help them start a rebellion—much less the hero, who could be called the mortal enemy of demons.

Judging by the testimonies of the refugees about the state of the demon realm, the contents of the letter are believable to a certain degree.

But it's just too unnatural.

Even if they really are plotting a rebellion because the new Demon Lord is too cruel a ruler, it's highly doubtful that they would want to ask for help from their enemies.

It's far more natural to assume that the letter is a trap in order to lure out the hero—me.

So we're going into this assuming it's a trap.

Of course, if we know it's probably a trap, the wisest course of action would be to ignore the invitation. There's no need to put ourselves in danger by showing up.

But we're risking it anyway, in case the demons really are in serious trouble and are asking us for help.

That's probably not the case, but from what we know about the situation on the other side of the border, it's not entirely outside the realm of possibility.

In the million-to-one chance that it's a genuine plea for help, if they really want us to aid them in overthrowing the Demon Lord, then I can't ignore that.

Besides, it could be a rare opportunity to lessen the animosity between humans and demons, if only a little.

The enmity between the humans and demons won't evaporate so easily, but it could be a chance to take a step toward peace.

I know I'm being overly optimistic.

That's just a fantasy, and in all likelihood, what's waiting for us is a trap.

But there is a slim possibility.

And I couldn't bring myself to throw that chance away.

"Yeah, I figured you'd say as much."

"If that is your choice, then of course I will follow you."

"Heh. You're a softy, but that's what's so great about you."

"If it's a trap, we'll deal with it, eh?"

My friends all kindly agreed to come with me.

I feel bad for bringing other people into it, too, but here we are, jumping into a trap.

"Ahhh, what the hell am I doing in this forest? I am a noble's daughter, even if I'm broke as hell, y'know? Where did I go wrong, huh?"

Aurel follows along glumly, muttering complaints.

Aurel and some empire soldiers have joined our usual group today, as well as a few adventurers, including Mr. Gotou.

Altogether, there are twenty of us.

It's enough people to proceed cautiously through the forest, keeping an eye out for traps without getting in one another's way.

The area designated for the meeting is deep in the forest, without a path to be found, so we're cutting through brush and forging our own way there.

"I'd like to give the damn idiot who picked this meeting place a piece of my mind."

"Perhaps they were trying to avoid being seen by the clans as well as the Demon Lord."

There are multiple clans living throughout the buffer zone, positioned wherever people might be able to pass through relatively easily.

Maybe an inaccessible place like this was the only way to avoid them.

And they probably had to keep away from the eyes of the Demon Lord, too.

"Huh?!"

I whirl around.

"Wh-what's the matter?" Yaana asks nervously.

I don't answer, staring into the depths of the forest.

But...there's nothing there?

"Julius, what's up?"

Noticing my strange behavior, Hyrince cautiously approaches.

Jeskan and Hawkin pull out their weapons and get into battle-ready formation.

"I felt like someone was watching us."

The others all follow my gaze, peering into the darkness.

"...Ain't nobody there."

Hawkin has the sharpest senses of all of us.

"...Maybe I just imagined it?"

"Don't be so sure," Jeskan warns. "Could be someone was sneaking around and ran away when you noticed them."

"We know this could be a trap. It doesn't hurt to be on the lookout for an ambush."

"Right."

We proceed more cautiously, keeping a close watch on our surroundings.

All conversation falls silent as we tensely make our way to the meeting place.

When we arrive, two people are there waiting for us.

One is a young boy and the other a woman.

A bewitching demon woman, wearing skimpy clothing that reveals her very ample bosom.

They're even bigger than Aurel's?!

"Glad you could make it!"

The female demon grins triumphantly and steps closer.

As I stand there frozen, she grabs my hand.

That was a failure on my part, I think.

My guard dropped while I was looking at her chest, even if it was only for a second.

It's in this moment that I recall what Jeskan said before about how I should build up a resistance to sexual provocations.

And that there are demons who specialize in that sort of thing.

"Guh?!"

Pain ripples through my body.

Immediately, I shake off the woman's hand.

Is this Poison Hand, the skill that's popular with assassins?!

But if it can break through my resistances and cause this much damage, it's no ordinary Poison Hand!

It could be the advanced skill Poison Attack or maybe even its evolved form, Deadly Poison Attack?!

"You're jumping us already?!"

Hyrince shoves his way between the female demon and me.

At the same time, the young male demon unleashes a magic spell.

Aurel counters it with a Fireball, and the spells cancel each other out.

"You think you can compete with MY magic?!" the boy demon shouts in surprise.

As if on cue, a large group of armed men emerges from the thicket and charges at us.

"Dammit! I knew it was a trap!"

"Attack! Don't let them get away!"

Jeskan readies his weapon, and the female demon shouts orders to the hidden soldiers.

We would have noticed such a large ambush before long—which is exactly why they're making the first move, to crush us before we get the chance to run.

"Hiyah!"

I cut down the first demon soldier who charges me.

Blood sprays through the air, and the soldier behind him stops as if rooted to the spot.

"Didn't you want to defeat the Demon Lord?!"

I knew they were lying from the beginning, but I can't help calling out to them anyway.

"As if we'd ever stand a chance!"

The response catches me by surprise.

The female demon isn't mocking me for being fooled or ignoring me—she's shouting back, as if in frustration at their hopeless situation.

"We have no choice but to obey! There's no turning back for us now!"

The female demon produces a whip and cracks it in the air.

Whips have a wide range of attack, but they're not as powerful as they look. If she combines it with Poison Attack, though, it becomes a lethal weapon that can poison anything it touches.

Hyrince blocks the oncoming whip with his shield.

"You really think these guys can be reasoned with?!"

He makes no effort to hide his irritation.

We were on guard for a trap, but we still didn't expect to be attacked so suddenly.

…No, I shouldn't make excuses.

I knew it was a trap, but I still carelessly let my guard down and approached the female demon, letting her get the upper hand.

That just means I have to make up for that blunder right away!

"Take this!"

I slash at one attacking soldier with my sword, then bring down another with a Fireball spell.

Then I loose a Light Sphere at the female demon.

"Gah?!"

She tries to deflect it with her whip, then grunts in surprise as the spell sends her whip flying and hurts her hand.

Clutching the injury, she takes a step back, and several demon soldiers move between us to shield her.

I couldn't finish her off…

"There's too many of them. Julius is in trouble… Tch! Retreat!"

As soon as he sees my condition, Hyrince calls for a retreat.

I took a lot of poison in that first attack. To be honest, I'm in serious pain.

Besides, we're vastly outnumbered, so our chances of winning this fight are slim.

"Jeskan! Give Julius a hand!"

"You got it! Come on, Julius!"

Jeskan supports me with his shoulder.

"Don't let them escape! We've got to bring them down here and now!"

The female demon shrieks at her men, still clutching her wounded hand, and they charge after us.

The young male demon keeps shooting magic at us, but Aurel has been consistently countering it.

Hawkin tosses one of his ace-in-the-hole magic items, stopping their charge. On top of that, Mr. Gotou swings his sword, and lightning crashes down on the enemy.

Amazing! So he has a lightning magic sword?!

"Withdraw! Now!"

Hyrince takes the lead, urging everyone to flee.

I start running as best I can with Jeskan's support, while Yaana runs alongside me, using Healing Magic to cure the poison.

With my last strength, I fire a wide-range Light Magic spell behind us.

It's not as powerful as Holy Light Magic, but unfortunately, I haven't learned a wide-range Holy Light Magic spell yet at my skill level. Even if I did know one, I'm not sure if I'd be able to use it properly in this situation.

"Dammit!"

Unable to wait and see if my spell did damage, I keep moving forward as Jeskan holds me up.

Yaana's magic seems to have rid me of most of the poison, but I haven't regained the health I lost.

As Yaana keeps casting Healing Magic on me while we run, my body starts to recover, but I can tell that I won't be able to fight any longer.

"Keep going! We're getting away!"

"Take this!"

I hear Hyrince shout from behind me, followed by Mr. Gotou's voice even farther back, accompanied by a thunderous rumble.

A flash of light follows behind us, then the belated sound of Mr. Gotou's magic sword attack ripping through the air.

"That's it! Keep running!"

Hyrince is bringing up the rear, but his voice sounds relatively close, so we must be succeeding in shaking off the enemy.

But it's still too soon to let our guards down.

I keep hobbling forward, hanging on to Jeskan for support.

But then...

"Huh?"

Maybe it was just my imagination.

I thought I saw something out of the corner of my eye.

But when I turn around, there's nothing there but trees.

"What's wrong?!"

"Sorry. It's nothing."

Jeskan casts me a glance, but I must have been seeing things.

There's no time to dwell on it right now, so I tell myself I imagined it and keep on running.

How could there be a bunch of dead men out in the woods strung up in white thread like grotesque decorations?

And a pure-white girl standing amid it all?

A vision like that doesn't make any sense.

I must have been hallucinating because of the poison.

Yes, I'm sure of it.

Thus, we managed to escape with our tails between our legs.

Fortunately, not a single person was lost, and I recovered quickly thanks to Yaana's healing.

Still, I have to admit it was a disaster.

"I'm sorry, everyone. I knew it was most likely a trap, but I still wasn't on my guard enough."

"It's fine," Hyrince reassures me. "They were really well prepared. We were ready for a trap, but when we showed up to talk and they immediately attacked us with poison, it was tough to react right away."

"But if I'd been more careful, maybe it wouldn't have happened. And on top of that, I slowed you all down afterward. I should be ashamed of myself as the hero."

"Oh, come on. It's our job as your friends to back you up when that happens, right?"

Jeskan pats me on the shoulder.

"But I made Hawkin use up a valuable magic item, too…"

"Those're made to be used, y'know? Ain't no point dyin' to conserve 'em." Hawkin smiles.

"And, Yaana, you had to heal me…"

"It's the saint's job to support the hero. I simply carried out my natural role."

If anything, Yaana looks happy she was able to help.

"You really saved us, Mr. Gotou."

"Nah, it's nothin'. If anything, thank this sword, not me."

Despite Mr. Gotou's modesty, I don't think we would have all gotten away unscathed if it wasn't for him and his sword.

Like Hawkin always says, tools are part of a person's strength.

"Thank you, too, Aurel. If you hadn't fended off that boy who seemed to be one of the leaders, we might've been in serious danger."

"Ahhh, it's no biggie. Honestly, running away after was the bigger pain."

It's so typical of Aurel that I can't help chuckling.

Yaana mutters something about "only because of those absurdly large bits of yours...!" but I'll pretend not to hear her...although it probably is hard to run with a chest like that.

In an effort not to look at the area in question, I glance around at everyone's faces instead.

Not a single one of them looks angry with me.

If anything, that makes it worse.

"...Why do I have to be so weak? Argh. I can't stand it!"

Instinctively, I clutch my scarf as tightly as I can.

I really am weak, like Master said.

No matter how hard I try, nothing ever seems to go right.

I'm not strong enough to make it happen!

I can't help but be frustrated and ashamed.

"Julius..."

Hyrince stands up and walks over to me.

Then he brings his fist down on my head.

"You damn moron!"

"Ow?!"

As I flinch and look up, Hyrince stares straight into my eyes.

"Listen, why do you always try to do everything on your own? Why do you put all the responsibility on your own shoulders?"

"Hyrince is right. We're your friends, aren't we? That means we're supposed to rely on one another. If one of us makes a mistake, another one of us just has to step in and help. I don't want you to save me all the time—I want us to save each other."

"Exactly. Do you remember the promise we made? I'm supposed to see that hopeful world of yours by your side, right, Sir Hero? By your *side*—not *behind* you. Or do you think I'm unworthy to fight beside you?"

"I am older than ya, too, y'know. You oughta try relyin' on your elders more, hey?"

"You guys..."

Hyrince, Yaana, Jeskan, and Hawkin.

They're my friends and comrades.

"If you can't do it on your own, we'll just have to do it together, right? Even if you're not strong enough alone, we'll be strong enough as a team. Take what just happened. You might not've stood a chance if you were alone, but we were with you. That's why we all made it back alive. You've got friends who want to fight at your side, see? So try to depend on us more."

Hyrince puts a hand on my shoulder.

I see... So even if I am weak, I have friends who will back me up.

"I'm...weak."

That truth hasn't changed.

On my own, I can barely do anything at all.

But if I'm with these trustworthy companions of mine, we can do so much more.

"But you'll stay by my side anyway?"

""""Of course.""""

The four of them all respond in unison.

As long as they're around, I'm sure I can accept my own weakness and keep moving forward.

Now I finally understand that.

"Awww, that was hella sweet."

"Aurel, come on—read the room."

Interlude   AN UNOPPOSABLE FORCE

Crunch. Crunch.

I shouldn't be able to hear it anymore.

But the wet, crunching sound keeps clinging to my ears.

Crunch, crunch, crunch, over and over.

"We blew it!"

I can't help yelling in frustration.

Our strategy was so haphazard that we were hoping to snag an empire leader or two, but instead we managed to land the hero, the biggest catch of all.

But then we let him slip right through our fingers!

If we'd succeeded, it would've been a big enough achievement to put all our trespasses behind us!

"Sanatoria, calm down."

"How am I supposed to calm down?! And how could you let a snot-nosed girl like that slow you down, Huey?!"

"I did the best I could! Besides, I didn't see you doing a single thing after that first surprise attack!"

Shouting at each other lets off some of the heat of our anger, and we both cool down a little.

"...I'm sorry. I went too far."

"No, I got overly heated, too."

We fall silent for a moment.

"So what are we going to do now?"

"…We'll just have to find another way to earn some points. We've got no other choice."

That's right: We're trying to curry favor and get ourselves in the Demon Lord's good graces.

Huey and I are actually commanders of the demon army.

We were born into good families and blessed with natural talents, and we put all that to work to earn our positions.

It hasn't exactly been a life of luxury, since the entire demon race is going through hard times, but we were luckier than the majority and satisfied with our lot.

But that all changed when the new Demon Lord appeared.

She wants to start up the war against humans again, no matter what it takes.

This is no joke. The demon race has already suffered so much from the incessant war that we can barely even get by as it is, you know.

We don't have the resources for another conflict, and whether we win or lose, the losses will be too great.

Our already bad situation is sure to get even worse.

I won't claim I did it for noble reasons like the sake of our race, like Balto or Agner.

I just didn't want to go to war or struggle any harder just to make ends meet.

That's why Huey and I agreed to our fellow commander Nereo's plan.

Little did we know that we were walking straight to our own doom.

We didn't want much—only to wipe out that awful Demon Lord.

One of the commanders, Warkis, took up the banner of revolution against the Demon Lord.

The rest of us aided him in secret, and when Warkis's army marched on the capital, we planned to join him and declare our open rebellion.

Between Warkis's revolutionary army and our own troops, we'd be able to outnumber the capital guards and defeat the Demon Lord.

At least, that was the plan.

But when push came to shove, the Demon Lord and her army sniffed out the rebellion and crushed it before Mr. Warkis could even finish gathering soldiers for the army.

And then Warkis committed suicide right before our eyes rather than be executed.

At the time, I thought I was still safe. I felt bad about Warkis, but I didn't think his death could possibly lead to my own.

But immediately after it happened, Agner gave us a warning, and we realized we were in far deeper trouble than we thought.

"I ask only that you be aware that you have been knowingly let off the hook. That Her Majesty the Demon Lord already has a knife to all your throats. Be assured that there will be no second chances if you make any strange moves again. The Demon Lord is not so benevolent as to look after those she does not need."

Agner is most likely the smartest person I know.

If he said the Demon Lord knew about us, then he must be correct.

That certainly put me on my toes.

And yet, even then, I still didn't understand just how terrifying the Demon Lord is.

Until I heard that crunching sound.

"I'm replacing the Ninth Army Commander."

The Demon Lord had summoned Huey; the Ninth Army Commander, Nereo; and me.

The Ninth Army currently exists only in name, with no actual troops.

Its only member is the commander, so it's not much of an actual position.

But the Demon Lord announced she was going to form a proper Ninth Army and change the commander.

"Black here will be taking over the Ninth. Play nice."

She introduced a man I'd never seen before, clad in black armor from head to toe.

A ridiculous outfit and a name to match. Obviously it must be a fake identity.

No doubt, this person is a friend of the Demon Lord's, who's getting the job thanks to nepotism.

But I did detect an aura of strength from the man.

It made sense for him to replace Nereo, who's better suited to internal administration.

And it's logical that the Demon Lord would want to have commanders she knows and trusts.

...I wasn't nearly as afraid as I should have been.

I should have realized something was wrong when she summoned just the three of us.

"Which means we won't be needing the current Ninth Army Commander anymore."

And that's when things went to hell.

A wet, crunching sound filled the room.

Nereo's head vanished from his neck.

His headless body collapsed to the floor before he could even react.

Blood gushed from his neck with the final pulses of his heart, staining the floor red.

Crunch, crunch, crunch.

With each successive crunching sound, another piece of Nereo's body disappeared.

Finally, the Demon Lord licked her lips, and the blood seeping into the floor was gone without a trace.

As if nothing had ever been there to begin with.

I thought I must be dreaming.

I *hoped* I was just dreaming.

But it was reality.

"Now, who will I need to replace next?"

The Demon Lord looked at us with a grin.

Ever since that day, the wet, crunching sound has clung to my ears.

It won't go away any more than the terror that accompanies it.

"Where's the other squad?"

"They haven't come back. We suspect they've been caught."

"How odd."

We sent a separate squad to go around and position themselves to cut off the hero's escape route.

If they were able to pin the hero and his party, we'd be able to catch up to them and attack from both sides.

How could our other squad have been wiped out before we even reached them?

"Perhaps they ran into each other while the hero was on his way here?"

As soon as I say it, I shake my head.

If the humans had encountered the other squad before they got here, surely they would've been more on their guard. Since my surprise attack succeeded, that mustn't be the case.

After our fight, the hero and the other humans wouldn't have been able to fight the other squad.

So by that logic, did our men run into a demon-hunting clan or something by chance and get wiped out before they ever encountered the hero?

"Either way, it'd be dangerous to stay here any longer."

Since the humans escaped, it's entirely possible that they'll send a big army back after us.

And if the other squad encountered a clan, they might attack us, too.

At any rate, we'd better withdraw.

"Let's get out of here."

"Are your hand and leg all right?"

"…No, not really. But I can still walk, so let's hold off on the healing until we get to a safe place."

My hand got broken in our fight with the hero and his little friends, and that last spell of the hero's injured my right leg.

It's not just me, either; the wide-range Light Magic attack exploded at our soldiers' feet, causing considerable casualties.

If it wasn't for that attack, we might've been able to chase them more effectively, but with so many of our soldiers unable to keep up on their wounded legs, we couldn't follow the fleeing hero for long.

They got us good, all right.

"…What should we do now?"

Huey's expression wavers anxiously.

"…Let's just focus on getting away for the time being."

I'm worried, too, of course.

We missed our big chance to take down the hero and failed to gain any merits, so now we'll have to find some other way to get into the Demon Lord's good graces.

Since she has her eye on us, we have no choice but to obey her every command and do whatever it takes to avoid being killed.

"Fortunately, since we carried out this plan in absolute secrecy, the Demon

Lord won't find out that we've failed. We didn't gain anything, but we didn't lose anything, either. Let's just call it a wash."

"Hmm. So getting soldiers killed for fun doesn't count as a loss? Iiiinteresting."

It can't be. How could I be hearing that voice right now?

At once, my entire body is paralyzed with fear.

The only movement I can manage is the occasional tremble.

Finally, praying that I was hearing things, I slowly turn around. If I move any faster, I'm afraid my injured leg will give out.

Once I turn, I see the last person I ever want to see, especially right now.

A seemingly young girl, kicking back in a luxurious chair that looks very out of place deep in the woods.

Though she appears too young to even be called a woman, on the inside, she's an unknowable monster.

It's the person we fear most: the Demon Lord.

"But…how?"

What is she doing here?

How did she find out? When and how did she get here?

I have so many questions and no answers.

All I know is that this might be the end.

"Hee-hee. I heard from White that you guys were up to something interesting, so I decided to come observe, that's all."

The Demon Lord smiles innocuously.

But I can tell that her eyes aren't smiling.

As soon as I heard the name "White," though, I understood everything.

White is a woman the Demon Lord brought in from somewhere, along with Black.

After the Demon Lord put Black in charge of the Ninth Army, she made White the Tenth Army Commander.

Black brought in the soldiers of the new Ninth Army, so I don't know who they are, but the new Tenth Army is even more mysterious.

Unlike the Ninth Army, the names on the Tenth Army list are people with real identities, but they all wear matching white clothes and look like completely different people from before.

There are rumors they've been brainwashed or hypnotized, which would be funny if it didn't seem like a terrifyingly real possibility.

And they all seem to be spies.

In other words, White is the Demon Lord's eyes and ears.

So the Demon Lord has been monitoring our actions through White...

"Our deepest apologies!"

While I stand there half-resigned to our fate, Huey bows deeply and starts apologizing.

"We had the hero backed into a corner, but he got away at the last moment, and we lost valuable soldiers in the process. I am truly sorry."

He earnestly acknowledges our failure, then goes even further.

"Great Demon Lord, Lady Sanatoria was really only helping me at my insistence. The Sixth Army initiated this strategy, so I will take full responsibility."

Huey looks like a child, yet here he is trying to act all cool and mature.

"Oh, it's fine. I'm not really mad about this or anything."

As Huey tries to take the blame, fully expecting his own death, the Demon Lord laughs it off carelessly.

Upon hearing this, Huey quickly raises his head.

It's incredibly cold here near the Mystic Mountains, yet his face is covered in a sheen of sweat.

I guess it's true that when people experience fear beyond their limits, they really do break out in a cold sweat.

But I would never mock him for this, because I'm in a similar state.

"Sure, it's annoying that you acted on your own, but whatever little pranks you get up to don't really matter much in the long run."

She's basically calling us insignificant, but instead of the humiliation I might normally feel, most of me is just relieved.

I'd rather her think of us as unimportant than see us as a hindrance.

I've heard that the old commander of the Ninth Army, Nereo, tried to dethrone the Demon Lord in secret even after Warkis's rebel army was quashed.

He got the Demon Lord's chef and an attendant on his side, and they tried to poison her.

This is all hearsay, but according to the rumors, the Demon Lord calmly ate the entire poisoned plate before saying this:

"Gross! Whoever made this disgusting meal is fired!"

The chef's head rolled the very next day—literally—along with the attendant who had conspired with them.

And Nereo, who was the mastermind behind it, was executed right in front of us.

I can still hear that crunching, smacking sound in my ears.

My appetite has been all but nonexistent ever since. The sound of my own chewing reminds me too much of that day.

I don't fully understand what happened, but one thing is for certain: Nereo was erased from this world by some horrible unknown force.

Since witnessing that, I now understand why Balto and Agner are so willing to obey the Demon Lord without question.

Both of them are deeply concerned for the future of the demon race, so it was strange that they would obey the Demon Lord, who seems hell-bent on destroying it.

But instead of realizing why, we let ourselves be fooled by the Demon Lord's youthful appearance, and we woke a sleeping dragon.

Those two must have already known that it's impossible to defy the Demon Lord.

Although it would've been nice of them to clue in the rest of us!

...No, I suppose Balto did try. Every time we met, he warned me not to attempt to rebel against her. I'm the one who let that fall on deaf ears.

I should've taken his warning more seriously.

I know there's no point dwelling on it now, but I can't help wishing I could turn back time and do things over again.

"Besides, you've already been punished for going behind my back."

The Demon Lord's words drag me harshly back to reality.

We've already been punished...?

What does that mean?

We're physically unharmed. Does that mean she did something else to us?

Beside me, Huey turns pale.

He has a younger brother.

Could she have done something to our families?!

My imagination starts to run wild.

"Y'know those guys you were saying haven't come back? That's 'cause I wiped 'em out already."

Though I hate to admit it, I feel a bit of relief on hearing that.

I feel bad for those soldiers, but I wouldn't have put it past the Demon Lord to do something far worse.

"So you don't need to apologize for losing valuable men, get it? I'm the one who did it in the first place."

Far from looking ashamed, the Demon Lord sticks out her tongue cutely, like a mischievous child.

How can she act like that when she's just massacred her own people?

Despite her cutesy actions, I can feel my blood running cold with fear of the Demon Lord.

And at the same time, something seems off.

Why would she wipe out that squad in the first place? It seems like an oddly indirect punishment.

Yes, from a military perspective, having those troops wiped out is a significant loss. But it doesn't punish Huey or me personally in any real way.

Does that mean she had a different goal, and punishing us was just an excuse?

Why would the Demon Lord need to destroy that squad?

"Erm, may I ask...why those soldiers...?"

The soldiers in the other squad were Huey's men from the Sixth Army, so I'm not surprised that he would have questions, but I'm still strangely impressed that he managed to speak up.

Maybe I'm getting emotional from the relief that we won't be punished any further?

"Sure. It'd be a pain for me if the hero died right now, so I had to get in your way a teensy bit."

Instead of growing angry as I feared, the Demon Lord answers calmly.

But I can't help being frustrated by her words.

"What?! But we set a trap to defeat the hero for you!"

Huey, you idiot!

What possessed you to defy the Demon Lord when she didn't seem too angry with us?!

"Yeah, see, this is why I don't want you doing stuff like this without permission. Although I guess we never really put out a notice not to go after the hero, so we'll call this one even, yeah? My bad."

"I don't believe it... So my troops died for such an arbitrary reason...?"

Huey hangs his head in disbelief.

Of course. To me they're just random soldiers, but Huey knew them as his subordinates.

I can't blame him for being shocked.

"Why don't you want the hero to be defeated?"

"You don't need to know that."

Huey was probably hoping to at least find out why his men had to die, but the Demon Lord curtly shuts him down.

"But...that's..."

Huey glances at the Demon Lord's expression, then swallows the rest of his words.

I'm sure that explanation didn't comfort him at all, but if he keeps pushing the Demon Lord for more information, her mood might turn sour.

He has no choice but to accept it, even if it doesn't make sense.

I inwardly sigh with relief when Huey backs down.

"This might not be much comfort to you, but they were fine soldiers."

"...Yes. Thank you."

I'm surprised the Demon Lord complimented the squad like that.

She seems to think of us all as nothing but expendable pawns, so I definitely wasn't expecting her to comfort Huey like that.

"They grew up nice and strong, and their deaths will make great fertilizer for the world. Yep. Some fine soldiers right there."

...Of course.

She really doesn't see us as people at all.

No wonder she said it might not be much comfort.

Huey clenches his fist.

"Hmm? You mad? Are you mad at me now?"

As the Demon Lord taunts him jokingly, I can see Huey gritting his teeth.

"Wait, calm down!" I hiss at him quietly.

It's all well and good if he wants to defy the Demon Lord and get himself killed, but not if I'm mixed up in it.

"Hey, guys. Did you know I came here all alone?"

The Demon Lord grins at us.

Now that she mentions it, I hadn't noticed in the shock of her sudden appearance, but there's no one else here with the Demon Lord—not even any guards.

It's just her and me, Huey, and the soldiers from the Sixth Army, although most of them were injured in the battle with the hero.

Which means we have her outnumbered.

"What do you wanna do?"

The Demon Lord tilts her head to the side inquiringly.

This certainly is a favorable situation, in theory.

The Demon Lord is more powerful than we can comprehend, but if she's on her own, we might be able to overcome her.

…As if I would ever entertain such a fleeting hope.

"A hilarious joke, Your Majesty."

I grab Huey's sleeve tightly while giving the Demon Lord my best ingratiating smile.

"I'm sure the soldiers would be proud to hear such high praise from the great Demon Lord. How could we possibly be angry? I should wish the same honor for myself one day."

No doubt she can see right through my bald-faced lies, but I have no choice but to try to smooth things over like this.

The Demon Lord's mouth quirks into a smile, so it seems like my strategy worked for now.

"Oh, good. Well, I look forward to seeing your work, then."

Does that mean she wants me to die and serve as "fertilizer for the world" like she said about those soldiers? Because if so, I'd rather not deliver on that.

"Of course."

But naturally, I have to agree to it out loud.

"Okay, White, let's head home."

The Demon Lord turns around.

There's a girl standing directly behind her, who's been there since who-knows-when.

A girl who's inhuman in a different way from the Demon Lord, her entire body white, as if all color has been bleached away.

She's so out of place in her surroundings that she looks like she stepped from a painting.

"All righty, we're gonna go back. No more funny business without my permission, 'kay?"

Or else I'll eat you.

With that, the Demon Lord and the girl in white disappear.

I wait a long while after their disappearance, then sink to the ground.

Only now do I finally feel the stinging pain from my wounded hand and leg.

But the reason I can't stand any longer has more to do with willpower than my injuries.

"All alone, indeed. Of course she had someone else with her."

I didn't even notice her lurking there.

But naturally, even if the Demon Lord really had been alone, I would've done the same thing.

We can't beat the Demon Lord.

No one can.

If we stood a chance, she wouldn't have shown up so casually and offered a challenge like that.

She was testing us.

What if we'd really tried to take her down?

I'm sure none of us would be alive by now.

The realization sets my body trembling.

It's cold.

So very, very cold, all the way down to my bones.

I'm terrified.

The only option we have left is total obedience to the Demon Lord, and even then, I don't know for sure if we'll survive.

The Demon Lord seems to be hoping we'll die, after all.

We can't rebel against her.

We're not strong enough. We'd simply die.

But even if we don't, we might very well die anyway.

"What are we supposed to do?!"

I choke the words out loud despite myself.

"Sanatoria. For now…for now, let's just get going."

Huey doesn't seem to have an answer, either.

Instead, he takes my hand and pulls me up, then puts his arm around my waist to help me walk.

As we move, my thoughts churn.

There's one force that no living thing can oppose: death.

Anything that lives must one day die.

And to me, the Demon Lord seems like an incarnation of death itself.

Sophia's Diary 10

Aah! Today's fresh blood is as tasty as ever!

You know what they say. It's unhealthy to repress your urges!

Huh? Too sudden?

What do you mean?

Awww, what? Don't drink blood?

But I *waaant* to.

Besides, whenever I drink a boy's blood, he looks super happy about it!

I get to drink blood, and he gets to enjoy it.

That's what you call a win-win situation!

The boys are starting to worship me a little, but that's not my fault.

Hmm? The class rep girl?

I guess Mr. Goody Two-shoes broke off their engagement and chased her out of the academy a while ago.

Serves her right!

Better yet, the other girls have all been on their best behavior ever since!

It's Sophia's time to shine!

Hmm?

A visitor at this hour...? Oh, it's White.

What's going on?

Waaaaah.

Master, I'm sorry. I was wrong.

Gaaah!

What is this?!

Did you curse me so I'm stuck calling you Master?

And if I disobey you, the curse forces me to sit?!

That's horrible!

What did I do wrong?!

Huh? I should figure it out myself?

...I can't think of a single thing!

Geh!

Hey, no need to get violent!

Hey, wait! Wha—?!

Stop!

Aaaaah!

Master, I'm sorry!

Just put me down!

You can't tie me to the ceiling in the nude!

We'll end up getting an R rating!

Huh?

Wait, why does it look like you're ready to leave?

What? Huh?

Are you going to leave me here like this?!

You've got to be joking, right?

Wait! WAIT!

I'm sorry; please forgive me; let me dooown!

At least allow me to put on some clothes!

J11   Julius, Age 17: Accomplishments

Soon, the whole world learned that I'd been attacked by demons.

The demon race was ending its long silence and going on the offensive.

Rumors spread like wildfire, and the empire began tightening its security at the border.

I started preparing myself so I'd be ready to run into battle at a moment's notice, too.

But the demons made no further movements, and time quietly went on.

"It's the hero!"

"Sir Hero is here!"

The excitement of the adventurers who came to greet me goes to show how desperate they are.

We've arrived in a wasteland near a certain village, where a simple base has been built.

Really, it's just a few tents with virtually no defenses, so it can hardly be called a base at all.

The adventurers are using this modest outpost to fend off a monster invasion.

"Now we'll be able to beat that earth specter!"

An earth specter is an earth-attribute variation of the spirit race of monsters, which is said to be nearly as dangerous as dragons.

The way these creatures live is very different from normal monsters. In fact, some say it's not even clear if they're living things at all.

They appear out of nowhere and produce small spirits, their underlings.

Then the small spirits gradually spread throughout the area, while the parent specter stays in place and keeps spawning more. Meanwhile, the unleashed minor spirits will start to attack any living creature they encounter.

This cycle continues indefinitely unless the specter is defeated.

On top of that, small spirits are considered C rank as soon as they're born, a danger level at which most average adventurers would form a party to defeat an individual monster.

And while even one small spirit requires that level of countermeasures, a specter can produce about ten small spirits a day.

If left alone for more than a week, that could easily be a big enough force to devour an entire town.

Thus, specters have to be defeated by adventurers or soldiers as soon as they're discovered.

Fortunately, since they produce so many small spirits, they're not hard to find. If anyone stumbles upon a small spirit, the parent is bound to be not too far away.

And for some reason, spirit monsters only appear in areas close to civilization.

If they started producing small spirits in an area far removed from any settlements, they might create a number of small spirits without being noticed, until it would be near impossible to defeat them, but that has never happened in recorded history.

Instead, they announce themselves as if asking to be found.

It's not known how spirit monsters are born, and they have certain features that make them seem like nonliving things, such as not needing to eat or sleep. Some people even believe that they're tests from the gods.

But I don't really care about the truth behind them.

As long as spirits are monsters that cause harm to people, I have only one course of action.

"What's the earth specter doing now?"

"It would be faster to show you than to explain. Come this way."

The person in charge here, a general from this nation who also participated in the anti-human-trafficking force, leads me outside the tent.

"Over there."

He points at a place so distant that it's barely a speck to the naked eye.

The earth specter is surrounded by countless small spirits.

It looks like a strange figure made out of rocks and dirt, like something inhuman making a creepy attempt to imitate one.

And it's surrounded by a swarm of small spirits—smaller than the parent but still vaguely humanoid.

However, since these ones are scrabbling around on all four thin limbs like insect legs, they look like an even more disturbing imitation of humanity.

At a glance, there are at least thirty.

"There's quite a lot of them."

"We've been fighting to try and reduce their numbers, but we can barely keep them from increasing. The soldiers and adventurers are getting exhausted, so it might be difficult to even keep that much up before long."

The general turns back toward the tent and heaves a sigh.

The tents are full of injured soldiers and warriors or others who are taking turns resting.

They all look visibly drained, and even the general himself looks far more haggard than when I last saw him.

The battle against the spirit will continue until the parent spirit is defeated, and it keeps producing small spirits all the while.

But the spirit itself is around the same danger level as a dragon: rank S.

This has to do in part with the small spirits that it continuously produces, but even on its own, the monster is not an enemy that can be taken down easily.

"Time is of the essence when fighting a spirit. Let's move out to defeat it right away."

There are adventurers and soldiers fighting the small spirits even now.

But no matter how many they defeat, the parent spirit will keep making more unless it's defeated itself.

The general and his forces are getting more and more exhausted, but the enemy can keep producing small spirits indefinitely.

"But you've just arrived, Sir Hero. Are you not tired?"

He suggests that we should rest first, since we arrived so late at night, but I shake my head.

"I'm sure you and the other people here are far more exhausted than I am from fighting for so long. It wouldn't be right for us to rest while you continue to battle. Right, everyone?"

I turn to the rest of my group.

"Fine by me."

"Of course!"

Hyrince and Yaana respond at once, and Jeskan and Hawkin nod mutely in agreement.

"All right, then let's go!"

Everyone else nods firmly.

"General, please gather anyone who can still fight. We'll charge in with everything we can muster."

"Understood!"

The fire returns to the haggard general's eyes.

I watch as he rushes over to the tents, then I head out toward the earth specter with my friends, helping others who are fighting small spirits along the way.

"Sir Hero?"

"It's the hero!"

"Hooray! Hooray!"

"Now we can win for sure!"

The people who were fighting the small spirits fall in step behind us.

They're deeply exhausted, yet they follow us with firm footsteps.

Now that the hero has joined the fight, they finally see a chance to win this endless battle.

That restores their fighting spirit.

"Everyone! I'm here! We're going to win this battle!"

I shout encouragement in order to raise their morale even further.

A chorus of war cries echoes through the wasteland.

I defeat one of the small spirits with a single spell.

Small spirits are C rank, so they'd pose a fair challenge to an ordinary adventurer, but my stats as the hero make it easy to defeat them.

And as I defeat more spirits along the way, the soldiers and adventurers who were busy fighting them all join us.

By now, we've almost reached the earth specter.

It seemed normal from the camp, but now that we've gotten close, I can see that it's easily three times the size of a human.

And there's a ring of small spirits protecting it.

"We'll deal with the earth specter! The rest of you, draw off the small spirits around it, but don't take on more than you can handle!"

I start weaving a spell as I call out orders.

Of all the monsters I've fought, the earth specter is second in danger ranking only to the likes of the phoenix and the Nightmare of the Labyrinth.

I can't hold back!

"Here we go!"

My wide-range light spell crashes into the earth specter and its surroundings.

I was hoping this might wipe out a bunch of the small spirits in the process, but no such luck—the earth specter countered my spell with Earth Magic.

It constructed the spell so quickly!

Ever since I embarrassed myself by walking into the demons' trap, I've been training whenever I have any time to spare.

I still can't compete with Master, of course, but my magic has gotten considerably stronger.

Yet, the earth specter was able to counter my spell in an instant.

One thing is for sure: This is going to be a tough fight.

The small spirits scatter toward us.

"Counterattack!"

As I call out to them, light envelops all our allies.

Yaana has cast support magic on them to temporarily raise their stats.

Hyrince moves in front with his shield at the ready and blocks the first of the small spirits.

"Raaah!"

The spirit slams into his shield, but he pushes it back.

Other small spirits make their way around Hyrince's shield, but Jeskan and I cut them in two.

At the same time, battles with the small spirits are breaking out all over the place.

"Keep pushing forward!"

"Right!"

Jeskan and I press onward toward the earth specter, defeating small spirits as we go.

The earth specter smashes a hand into the ground and grabs the giant boulder that emerges.

"Look out!"

Just as Jeskan shouts, the earth specter flings the boulder toward us.

It's huge—huge enough to flatten our bodies easily.

I launch a Holy Light Sphere at the giant boulder.

The balls of rock and light crash into each other and explode.

Hyrince uses his shield to fend off the small rock fragments that fly toward us.

We keep moving forward, closing the distance between us and the earth specter.

The earth specter seems to realize that it can't defeat us with boulders and smashes both its hands into the ground, shaking the entire area.

For a spirit that manipulates earth, causing a local earthquake is no challenge at all.

Some of the soldiers and adventurers tumble over or fall to one knee.

While my companions and I don't lose our balance, we do stop moving.

Then the earth specter's arm swings toward us from the side.

"Hyrince!"

"Guh?!"

Hyrince, who was spearheading the group, gets sent flying, along with his shield.

"Bastard!"

Jeskan takes this opportunity to get up close to the creature's legs and swing his ax at its shin.

"Eh?!"

But his ax makes only a shallow cut before it stops.

This thing is tough!

"Hunh?!"

The earth specter deals a sharp kick to Jeskan, sending him flying just like Hyrince.

Then I bring my sword down toward the monster's head.

While the earth specter was focused on Hyrince and Jeskan, I used Dimensional Maneuvering to get above it and prepare one big strike.

But the earth specter raises its hand to protect its head from my sword.

See if I care!

"Aaaargh!"

My sword fills with the power of holy light.

Then it slices the earth specter's arm right off and plunges into its head.

The earth specter topples backward, hitting the ground with an enormous rumble.

But that wasn't enough!

The earth specter is still alive.

I have to finish it off while it's still down!

As I career toward the ground, I take my sword in my other hand, pointing it down toward the creature for the finishing blow.

The earth specter swings its remaining arm toward me.

"Julius!"

Hyrince's shield and Jeskan's ax block the arm together.

They both threw their weapons simultaneously to try to stop its attack. However...

"Oof!"

The earth specter's arm doesn't stop, and it smacks me down hard.

I hit the ground once, then bounce back upward. As that happens, I activate Dimensional Maneuvering and manage to land on my feet.

"Urk..."

As I cough violently, the taste of blood fills my mouth.

I should've known it wouldn't be that easy.

The earth specter uses its intact arm to right itself.

Its other arm has been cut off, and its head has a deep fissure on the top.

The monster's definitely taken a lot of damage, too.

I guess we're about even.

But then my entire body feels better all at once.

It's Yaana's Healing Magic!

She's been behind us with Hawkin all this time, but she must have cast Healing Magic on me from a distance.

Thank goodness! Now I can do this!

The earth specter swings one of its legs upward.

Is it planning to use its leg to cause an earthquake now that it's missing one arm?!

"Not gonna happen!"

Jeskan's sickle and chain wrap around the other leg, the one keeping it upright.

"Heave-ho!"

Then Jeskan and Hyrince pull on the chain with all their might.

Since it was standing on one leg, the earth specter pitches sideways, about to fall.

While it tries to recover, I shoot four Holy Light Spheres at it.

Simultaneously firing multiple spells—the biggest attack I can do right now.

"Gooo!"

The four balls of light crash directly into the unbalanced earth specter, knocking its body backward instead.

The monster crashes down onto its back again.

This time, its body breaks apart, and it shows no signs of standing up again.

"Did we win?"

A voice breaks the silence, followed by others.

"We won!"

"We wooooon!"

Cheers erupt around the battlefield.

I raise my sword toward the sky. "Come on! Let's clean up the rest of these small spirits!"

Forcing back the desire to collapse on the spot, I focus my energy on getting rid of the rest of the spirits.

Some belated reinforcements come to join us, and before long, we've wiped out every last small spirit.

We carry the giant remains of the earth specter back to the village, where we're greeted by a chorus of cheers from the villagers.

Now these people are free from the threat of the earth specter.

That thought instantly puts a smile on my face.

"Here, Mr. Hero!"

I turn around to find a little girl offering me a flower.

"Is this for me?"

I crouch down to her eye level and accept the flower—just an ordinary wildflower, the sort you could find anywhere.

"S'all peaceful here now thanks to you, Mister!"

"Thank you."

To me, the little girl's words and the flower she gives me in gratitude are worth more than the most expensive bouquet.

It makes me feel like what I've done wasn't for nothing.

"You're so cool, Mr. Herooo!"

As I gaze at the flower, a boy suddenly pushes aside the little girl and jumps in front of me.

"You beat that thing, right?! How can I get strong like you, huh?!"

The boy points excitedly at the remains of the earth specter and looks at me eagerly.

I know that boys his age admire strength, but...

"You can't."

"Huh?!"

Brushing the boy off with a cold response, I walk past him and kneel next to the girl he pushed aside, who's sitting on the ground crying.

"That must've hurt, huh? Don't worry—I'll heal you."

I pat her head gently and use Healing Magic to fix up her scrapes.

"There, all better."

"Really?"

"Uh-huh. You're okay now."

"It stopped hurting! Thank you!"

The little girl stops crying.

"Kids who hurt the people close to them can't get strong."

I turn back to the boy, who's standing there stunned.

"I'm sure you want to get strong enough to beat monsters like that one," I say, gesturing to the earth specter. "But if you use that strength to make people cry, you're not really strong at all. That's a bad thing. You made this girl cry, and that was very unkind of you."

"Oh..."

"Strong people don't make anyone cry. Only bad people do that. You can't be strong acting this way."

He might be too young to understand what I mean, but he needs to know that it's wrong to do bad things.

"Now, since you were bad, you have to apologize."

"Weh…"

"Don't you know that a hero has to defeat bad people? So if you're going to be bad…"

"I'm sorry!"

I ended up threatening him a little, but the boy finally apologized.

"Good. Just like that. As long as you don't do bad things, I'm sure you'll get nice and strong."

"Really?"

"Uh-huh. But if you forget that and do more bad things, I'll have to come defeat you, so remember to be good, okay?"

"'Kay."

After that, the boy and girl make up and walk away holding hands.

"I guess teaching kids to be good is one way to stop evil from happening, like you said way back when."

Jeskan smiles as he watches the children leave.

"It might not be the kind of strength that boy was looking for, but I'd be happy if he can be strong enough to walk the straight and narrow instead of turning to crime."

"True."

I've traveled all over the world, defeating monsters, bandits, and so on.

Those things have meaning on their own, of course, but I think I can have a small effect by showing people what kind of hero I am, too.

Hopefully, that'll turn out to be a good influence.

J12   Julius, Age 21: Family

"Welcome home, big brother."

I'm back in the royal castle for the first time in ages.

There, I find my half brother Leston, the third prince and son of the king's second concubine.

The king's wife, the true queen, holds the most influence, followed by the first and second concubines. My mother was the third concubine, so she had the lowest position of them.

If I weren't the hero, I might have even been in a lower position than Leston.

It's a strange thing to think about.

"Thank you. Here, a souvenir."

"Ooh. Thank you! Is this a magic sword from the empire?!"

Leston gazes happily at the sword I handed him.

It's a magic sword imbued with the power of fire, similar to the one I borrowed from my master once.

Magic swords are valuable as it is, but this one also has a unique origin, so it wouldn't be sold on the open market.

However, rumors have spread about them, since high-ranking empire officials are often seen carrying them.

Rumors say that the empire has succeeded in mass-producing magic swords.

I asked Master about it when I last saw him, but he artfully dodged the subject, so I don't know the truth.

But since I was able to acquire magic swords like this as a result, I can't really complain.

"But are you sure it's okay to give me something like this?"

"It's fine. I actually have a few more of the same kind."

I still have several other magic swords. I'd joked to Master that I wanted one, and he promptly responded, *"Well, I'm not using 'em,"* and gave me no less than ten.

Master can be surprisingly generous.

"Well, they come from a somewhat unfortunate source," he said at the time. *"But they're still fine weapons."*

I don't know what he meant, but there must be some strange story behind them, because Master seemed awfully eager to be rid of them.

That must be why he gave me such valuable items so readily, even though you could easily make a fortune by selling even one.

I gave Hyrince an incredibly sturdy one that can recover from damage on its own, though it doesn't have any special offensive effects.

Jeskan got a broadsword with a special flame effect.

For Hawkin, there was a short sword with lightning and paralyzing effects.

And for myself, I chose a sword that, like Hyrince's, doesn't have any special attacks but conducts magic exceptionally easily and is helpful for support while using spells.

Unfortunately, there weren't any weapons well suited to Yaana, but our fighting strength increased dramatically with all these new weapons.

I wasn't sure what to do with the remaining six swords, but I decided to give five of them to my family members: Father, Cylis, Leston, Shun, and Sue.

I already gave Father and Cylis theirs.

Father seemed happy, but my elder brother's expression looked dour.

It seems like we're doomed to keep growing further apart.

I want to do something about it, but since I'm away from home so frequently, we don't have many chances to interact. I think my only choice is to keep trying to get him to open up little by little over time.

We were relatively close when we were kids, so I'm sure we can learn to understand each other again.

As for Shun and Sue, I decided to wait to give them theirs until they graduate from the academy.

If they get accustomed to having such strong weapons this early, they could grow overly dependent on them. Knowing those two, I doubt that would happen, but I prefer to be on the safe side.

Besides, they'll make good graduation gifts.

...I'm not just hesitant to give the swords to them because I might not be able to beat them in a sparring match anymore, all right?

Really. I swear.

"Come to think of it, Mr. Potimas mentioned something about holy swords, not magic swords."

"Holy swords?"

Most swords with special effects and properties are called magic swords, but those with the power of light are called holy swords. They're considered special, even compared to other magic weapons.

"Something about a special holy sword that's been in the royal family here for generations. I've never heard anything about it, have you?"

"No, I don't think so."

Father or my elder brother might know something, though.

It could be a secret that's known only to the king.

But then why would an outsider like Potimas know about it?

Mr. Potimas is an elf who's staying here in our kingdom as an ambassador of the elves.

I've never actually seen him for myself, but Leston seems to be developing a friendship with him.

Mr. Potimas's daughter goes to the same academy as Shun and Sue, and I'm told they're good friends.

The elves are a race that extolls world peace and often devotes themselves to charitable causes.

For some reason, though, they don't work with the Church of the Word of God, and since I technically am part of the Church, I never really interact with them.

Although, since their goals seem to align with mine, I'd like to get to know them if I can.

Leston has apparently been investing in and even directly helping the elves with their activities.

"Where did Mr. Potimas hear about that?"

"Who knows? Elves live a really long time, though, so maybe it's just an old legend."

It could be that our ancestors used to pass down a holy sword long ago, but it's since been lost, or something like that.

"Or he might've believed a false rumor."

People often make up stories about the royal family, frequently suggesting that they have a vast hidden treasury or something of the like.

Most of those rumors are fake, so it could be that Mr. Potimas heard some such misinformation.

"Although it was really specific, so I'm not quite sure."

"Oh? How so?"

"You know how there are those stairs in the castle that go down but don't lead anywhere? There's been chatter about how if a worthy person goes down there, a door will open or something. Those stairs really are mysterious, so it'd be kinda cool if it was true, huh?"

Leston is right: There certainly is a mysterious staircase in the castle.

It goes downward but only leads to a wall.

There's no hidden room or anything, so it's a mystery why those stairs exist.

In that way, it's definitely the kind of thing that rumormongers would love to spread stories about, but most people don't even know it exists.

Because the only way to get to the mysterious staircase is through the royal family's private quarters.

And of course, most people wouldn't approach a staircase that doesn't go anywhere.

Even the servants who are allowed in the private chambers rarely set foot near the steps, so most people don't know they exist at all.

The only people who know are mostly royalty, and it's rarely discussed, since nothing is known about it.

I had forgotten they existed at all until this conversation.

"But it's probably false, 'cause I didn't find anything there."

"So you went?"

"I mean, how could I resist?"

So Leston went to the stairs after hearing this story, but he didn't find anything.

"Oh, I know! Since you're here, you should try it, too!"

Leston claps his hands together once, like he's hit on a brilliant idea.

"You're royalty *and* a hero. Who could be more worthy than you?!"

"Yeah, right. That's so unrealistic."

"What's wrong with being a little unrealistic? You're free right now, aren't you? Come on—humor me for a bit!"

"All right."

Leston doesn't seem willing to take no for an answer, so I decide to give in without a fight.

Since I see my half brother so rarely, there's no harm in going along with his request.

"Great! Let's head there right now, then!"

"Okay, okay."

Leston bounces out of the room, and I follow him with a wan smile.

We walk through the royal family's private chambers and reach the staircase within.

Leston starts down the stairs into the darkness without hesitation.

"Come on! Hurry!"

"I'm right behind you."

I can't help smiling at Leston's somewhat childish behavior for his age.

He's actually a lot sharper than he might seem, but he puts on a clownish act to avoid drawing the true queen's eye so she won't consider him a potential threat to his older brother's position.

…Although I don't think all of it is an act.

He's smart, but he also has an irrepressible childlike curiosity.

I use magic to light the way as I follow Leston down the long stairway.

When I was a child, I explored around here with my elder brother, too.

We were so sure that we would discover a hidden door or something of the sort.

In the end, of course, we found no such thing, but it's a fond memory now that my brother's grown so distant.

As I reminisce, we reach the bottom of the stairs.

It's a dead end, with nothing there but a wall.

"Come on, big brother!"

Leston prompts me to step up to the wall.

Nothing's going to happen, you know…

Or so I thought.

"Huh?!"

The wall that was there just seconds before disappears like it was a mirage.

And instead, there's a small room up ahead.

"Huh? For real?"

Leston is as surprised as I am.

As a child, I didn't find anything when I searched around down here for a hidden door.

My father chuckled afterward and told me, *"I did the same thing when I was your age. Boy, was I ever disappointed when I didn't find anything."*

If what he said then was true, then he doesn't know about this room, either.

"Th-this is huge!"

Leston's voice trembles with excitement.

But I'm already focused on the object enshrined in the center of the small room.

It's a sword.

A sheathed sword, standing on a pedestal.

"Is that the holy sword?"

"It must be!"

Leston starts to dash toward it.

"Ah! Wait!" I grab his hand and pull him back.

"Come on—what's the matter?!"

"Something's there."

Ignoring Leston's protests, I keep my gaze fixed on the pedestal.

"Oh-ho?"

Behind the pedestal is a gorgeous sculpture of a white dragon.

It's small, about the same height as the sword.

And right now, it's starting to move.

"A child, eh? Thou comest here knowing nothing of this place. But it appears thou art worthy."

It's not a statue!

It's a tiny white dragon.

But in spite of its small size, it has an aura of immense power.

Like the phoenix I once saw—no, even stronger!

It might even be on par with the infamous Nightmare of the Labyrinth.

But since it's speaking to me in my language through Telepathy, that means we can communicate. And it doesn't seem like it's about to attack us.

Hopefully we can resolve things by talking to each other.

"Who are you?"

"*I am the light dragon Byaku, guardian of the Sword of the Hero.*"

"The Sword of the Hero?"

"*Indeed.*" The dragon called Byaku nods sagely. "*Hero, thou hast the right to wield this sword. What shall thou doest?*"

"I'm not sure how to answer that…"

I don't even know what kind of weapon this so-called Sword of the Hero is.

In fact, I'm still not really sure what's going on here.

"*If the hero wields it, it has the capacity to cut down even a god in one strike, but it can only be used once. What would you cut with this sword?*"

"…It can really cut anything?"

"*Verily.*"

"Even a legendary-class monster?"

"*With ease,*" the dragon confirms. "*Even I would be powerless before this sword.*"

I don't know how powerful Byaku the light dragon is, but I can tell that I wouldn't stand a chance of winning if I challenged it to battle.

But it says that this sword could easily defeat it.

If that's true, how absurdly powerful must that sword be?

For a moment, the image of a white spider flashes across my mind.

If I had this sword, could I defeat even the Nightmare of the Labyrinth?

"No."

I shake away the thought.

The Nightmare of the Labyrinth hasn't appeared since that day, so there's no point thinking about it now.

I can't bring the victims of the Nightmare back to life.

"*What would you cut? Or whom?*"

"Nothing. And no one."

I know my answer.

I won't use this sword to cut anyone or anything.

"This sword can only be used once, right?"

"Indeed."

"Then I won't rely on it for anything."

"Oh-ho?"

The light dragon Byaku looks at me with great interest.

"There is little peace to be gained by cutting down one thing or one person. And I don't think it would be worth the cost."

For instance, what if I used it to cut down an evil king?

With the tyrant overthrown, perhaps the nation would know peace.

But not for long.

All manner of other trials would await that nation afterward.

They would need a new leader, or leaders, to take over the government.

They would need retainers to support these leaders.

And they would need citizens to support the government.

Even if the king was cut down, true peace could be obtained only through the hard work of the people left alive. And even then, given enough time, a similar king might appear.

But this time, there would be no sword.

So what would be the point?

"There's no point unless I accomplish things with my own hands and continue to uphold those accomplishments."

"Even if wielding this sword might save your life one day?"

"I won't deny that."

I can't help wondering what would have happened if I'd had this sword when I encountered the Nightmare of the Labyrinth.

But I still don't think that all the unhappiness in this world can be solved with a single wave of some magic sword.

"I am weak; I know."

I'm painfully aware of that fact.

"But I have friends who support me. So I can keep fighting, even if I am weak. There have been many times when I wished I was stronger. But true strength doesn't come from depending on a weapon that can only be used once."

I put a hand on my scarf.

I think what I really need is the strength to keep on fighting.

There is so much injustice in the world.

But I want to be strong enough to keep on fighting and chasing my ideals, no matter what.

So I don't need this destructive power.

"*I see, I see. How admirable!*"

Suddenly, Byaku emits a flash of light.

I close my eyes automatically, and when I open them again, the light dragon is nowhere to be found.

"Where did you go?"

"*I am right here.*"

I look toward the source of the Telepathy, but nothing is there.

Nothing except the sword on the pedestal.

"*I've merged with the sword. Take it with you.*"

"What? Um, weren't you listening to me?"

I'm pretty sure I just said I don't need it…

"*I was indeed. That is why you must take it. You are the one who most deserves this sword.*"

"Erm…"

Oh dear.

"*I shall seal the power of the sword and enter a deep slumber. If you should ever need my power, and the power of the sword, simply call upon me.*"

Does that mean I have to take the sword with me now?

I guess I don't have a choice, since I'm a little scared of refusing.

"*A man such as you might even be able to save a god instead.*"

With that, the telepathic connection abruptly cuts off.

I hesitate for a moment but end up taking the sword with me.

It doesn't look like it has the unspeakable power Byaku described, though perhaps that's just because it's sealed.

"Whoa. That was amazing, big brother!"

Leston, who watched these events unfold in silence, suddenly crows triumphantly.

"Leston, you mustn't tell anyone else about this."

I hate to detract from his excitement, but this is very serious, so I have to sternly warn him.

A holy sword that has the single-use power to defeat even a legendary-class monster?

If people knew I had such a thing, it would cause an unnecessary uproar.

"All right. I swear on the gods that I won't tell a soul."

Leston grows serious, apparently realizing the same thing, and solemnly agrees.

"Okay. Let's go back, shall we?"

We leave the room and head back up the stairs.

As soon as we exit, the area where the sword was kept turns back into an ordinary wall.

The next day, that same sword is hanging at my waist.

The light dragon Byaku hasn't tried to communicate with me via Telepathy again. I haven't even sensed its presence, to the point where I wonder if it really merged into the sword at all.

And the sword itself seems like an ordinary sword, without a hint of special powers.

But the fear that I might accidentally unleash its real power somehow prevents me from wielding it, so I still plan to use my regular magic sword.

That means I'm carrying two swords at all times, but I don't think I have much of a choice.

"You gonna learn two-sword style or what?"

Hyrince greets me as we meet up in the castle.

"It's just a spare. I thought I should start carrying one, like Jeskan."

"Oh, gotcha."

Hyrince accepts my excuse, since Jeskan really does carry around multiple weapons all the time.

"We're going to the academy today, right?"

"Yeah."

The demons have finally started to make unusual movements, so the plan is to head to the empire. I don't know when I'll be able to come back.

In the worst-case scenario, if the war with the demons starts, I might not even make it back at all…

So I want to spend time with my family before I go.

My exchange with Leston yesterday was part of that plan.

Today, I'm going to the academy to meet up with Shun and Sue.

As Hyrince and I walk through the castle, a man approaches us.

He has pointed ears—an elf.

There's only one elf in this kingdom who can enter the castle. This must be Mr. Potimas, the one who's been spending time with Leston.

"Hrm?"

Mr. Potimas stops in front of us and looks at me appraisingly.

His gaze pauses on the holy sword at my waist, then shifts to Hyrince next to me.

"...Hmm. Well, no matter."

Without any further comment, he passes by us and keeps walking.

"...What's up with the attitude?" Hyrince grumbles, watching him go.

Considering that I'm a member of the royal family, he certainly didn't show proper manners.

But I'm hardly one to talk in that department, because I was glaring at him the whole time.

I'm not exactly sure why I took that attitude toward him myself.

For some reason, though, I felt instinctively that he was no friend of mine.

"We should advise Leston and my father to rethink their involvement with that man."

"Uh, sure."

Hyrince seems bewildered by my harsh reaction, since I'm not normally one to concern myself with how other people treat me.

I'm still unsure where these intense feelings are coming from, too.

But that man is definitely bad news.

Of that I have no doubt.

"Hyrince."

"What's up?"

"If...if I ever die and you survive, I want you to give this sword to Leston."

Again, I don't know what's compelling me to say this, but I feel like I have to.

"Whoa, don't say stuff like that."

"I know. I don't intend to die before you, of course. I just felt like I ought to tell you."

"Don't worry. I told you I'm not gonna let you die before I do, remember? So I can't help you with that sword thing."

"Right. Of course."

Maybe my thoughts just turned dark because of the mysteriously ominous sense I felt from that man.

We arrive at the academy and wait for Shun and Sue in the visiting room.

Before long, Shun bursts through the door excitedly.

"Brother!"

Sue follows him in and quietly closes the door behind them.

Something about her behavior seems strange to me.

Sue has always been the quiet type except when Shun is involved, but was she always this intensely silent, as if she's holding her breath?

"Shun, Sue, good to see you."

"It's great to see you, too!"

"Mm."

Shun responds happily to my greeting, while Sue's response is short.

"Nice to see you again, too, Mr. Hyrince."

"Yeah, you too. You've grown a bunch again since last time I saw you."

After exchanging greetings with Shun, Hyrince steps back, as if to relinquish the spotlight to me.

"Have you been doing all right?"

"Yes."

Already, Shun's weathered assassination attempts and even a wyrm attack at his school.

When I heard about that, I was so worried that I could barely stand it, but apparently, he's happily enjoying his school life now.

"And you, Sue?"

"Mm."

I try conversing with Sue, too, but she isn't giving any real responses.

"Sue, are you feeling under the weather?"

"Mm-mm." Sue shakes her head, but she's obviously acting strange. "I'm fine."

"…If anything's bothering you, you can tell me, okay?"

"Mm."

Sue nods, looking almost on the verge of tears.

"Shun, make sure you're looking after her, all right?"

"Yes, of course."

Shun nods obediently, as if he has some concerns about Sue's behavior, too.

"I want to help, but I have to go to the empire soon. So you'll have to take good care of each other."

"The empire…because of the demons?"

Evidently, word about the demons' strange activities has even reached the academy.

"Yeah. So I don't know when I'll be able to come back next."

"I'm sure you have nothing to worry about, big brother, but please be careful."

Shun looks at me with such complete faith that I'm a little embarrassed.

I'm not as strong as he thinks I am…

"Do you really have to fight the demons?" Shun's face clouds. "Why do they want a war so badly? I don't understand it."

"Good question."

I don't want to fight, either.

Shun is so strong and talented that people call him a prodigy, but he's still grown up as a kind boy who's averse to fighting.

It's my hope that he'll live his life without ever having to put his strength to use, but I know how difficult that would be, too.

"I don't know why the demons insist on starting a war, either."

In the back of my mind, I remember the female demon shouting that they have no choice but to obey the Demon Lord.

The demons have their reasons for fighting, too.

"But if they intend to threaten our peaceful lives, we have no choice but to oppose them."

Either way, we need to fight.

"It'd be ideal if we could settle things without fighting. If it was possible to make peace with the demons, then of course I'd rather do that. But the reality is that things aren't so easy."

Shun looks down sadly as I go on.

"But I do think that we'll never get anywhere if we keep using that as an excuse."

"Huh?"

I know most people would laugh at me and say I'm naive.

But even so…

"I know I'm just dreaming. I don't care if people laugh at me for being unrealistic. But there's nothing wrong with having a goal to strive for. Mine is a world where everyone can live happily in peace. And I'll keep chasing that ideal until I die."

"Brother…"

"…!"

Sue jumps up and runs out of the room, as if she can't bear to hear my words any longer.

"Ah! Sue?!"

Shun turns around in alarm.

"It's okay. Go after her."

Sue isn't acting like herself right now.

I'm sure she needs Shun's help.

"But…"

Shun hesitates, knowing he won't be able to see me again for a while.

"I'll come back to visit once things calm down."

"…Promise me!"

"I promise. See you soon."

"Right!"

With that, Shun runs out of the room after Sue.

"That wound up being a short good-bye."

Hyrince shakes his head, but I respond with firm resolve.

"Well, I'll just make sure the next visit is much longer. I promised. I'll come back no matter what."

"…Yeah. You're right, of course."

"Let's all come back together."

I leave the academy with renewed determination.

I do not want to fight.

But there are times when one has no other choice.

For the sake of true worldwide peace.

"Here we go."

I will fight, in order to win peace for this world

with my own hands.

I do not want to fight.

But there are times when one has no other choice.

For the sake of true peace.

"Here we go."

I will fight, in order to win peace for this world

with my own hands.

KINGDOM CALENDAR 856
JULIUS, AGE 22
OUTBREAK OF THE GREAT HUMAN-DEMON WAR

TIMELINE Kingdom History

Year 834 The second prince of Analeit Kingdom, Julius, is born to the king's third concubine.

Year 840 Julius becomes the hero.

Year 841 The fourth prince of Analeit Kingdom, Schlain, is born to the king's third concubine.

The king's third concubine passes away.

Year 842 Julius encounters the Nightmare of the Labyrinth during the Tragedy of Zatona.

Julius takes part in the Defense of Keren County against the white-spider swarm.

Julius becomes Ronandt's apprentice.

Year 843 Julius sustains near-fatal wounds during Ronandt's training.

Year 844 Yaana is tentatively appointed saint.

Year 845 The anti-human-trafficking force is formed by the Word of God Church.

Yaana officially becomes the saint.

Hyrince becomes Julius's attendant.

Year 846 The force begins its activities.

Jeskan and Hawkin join the force.

Year 847 Schlain and Suresia undergo the Appraisal ceremony.

Tiva perishes.

The force is disbanded.

Year 848 Julius, Hyrince, Yaana, Jeskan, and Hawkin defeat monsters and criminals in various lands.

Year 849 Julius attends the migration of the phoenix.

Year 850 Julius is caught in a demon trap and attacked but manages to escape.

Year 851 Julius defeats the earth specter.

Julius defeats one Nightmare's Vestige in the Great Elroe Labyrinth.

Year 852 Julius defeats a greater fire wyrm.

Year 853 Julius resolves an excessive monster outbreak in Oigi Dungeon.

Year 854 Julius wipes out a swarm of mutated Potoloa infesting the Western Great Kakura Forest.

Year 855 Julius acquires the Sword of the Hero in a hidden room in Analeit Castle.

Year 856 The Great Human-Demon War begins.

AFTERWORD

This is Okina Baba, reporting live on the scene and so forth and so on.

Here we are at Volume 11.

Two of the same number—a repdigit.

People love repdigits for some reason and place a kind of special value on them.

Honestly, even I get excited about repdigits.

And since this repdigit volume is coming out at the beginning of the new Reiwa era, it feels like an especially auspicious occasion.

Yet, in order to get a repdigit, you need to reach two digits first.

And to reach the next repdigit, Volume 22, I would need to double the amount of volumes I've put out so far.

In fact, I suspect that this series might be over before we reach the next repdigit.

If not, I'm sure I'll go on about repdigits again in the afterword of Volume 22.

Maybe I should even aim for the next repdigit to be the last volume?

Although, as a creator, I do feel like a repdigit or a multiple of five is always a good number for the last volume of a series.

Realistically, I think it would be difficult to end this series on the next repdigit.

I don't even know if it's going to last until the next repdigit.

Did I mention 11 is a repdigit?

*　　*　　*

Now, Volume 11 is totally different from the previous volumes.

There have been previous volumes with a different tone or format than usual, true.

But I don't think any of them has been as distinct as this one.

This series has gone on long enough to break two digits and even reach a repdigit, but now I've gone and made an unbelievable blunder in this volume.

The protagonist barely shows up at all.

Where is the titular spider content? Where?!

There's such a huge lack of spiders that they should probably change the title just for this volume!

What the hell is the author thinking?

Oh, that's me.

Yes, the protagonist of this volume is Julius the hero, older brother to our reincarnated friend Shun.

There have been plenty of other narrators besides the protagonist thus far, but this is the first time that we don't get the protagonist's point of view a single time in the entire volume.

And instead of being someone close to the protagonist, the narrator is someone who's both physically and mentally very far removed from her.

But I think that by distancing ourselves from the protagonist, we get to see things that she would never have mentioned, things that the protagonist knows but other people don't, and even some things that the protagonist doesn't know about at all.

And then there's that final scene!

It would never have been completed without my editor W and the talented Kiryu.

Which brings us to the thank-yous.

Thank you to Tsukasa Kiryu for the excellent illustrations as usual.

I think anyone who read this book to the end will see how wonderful that last scene is.

So wonderful! So beautiful! Really, thank you so much!

Thank you to Asahiro Kakashi for your hard work on the manga.

In Volume 7, which goes on sale at the same time as this novel volume, you'll get to see even more of dear old Ronandt and his explosive sayings!

I'm impressed as always with the characters' expressions that you don't get to see in the novels.

And thank you to the anime staff as well.

They're all hard at work as we speak, so please wait for more information.

Thank you to my editor W and everyone else who assisted with the production of this book.

And to everyone who picked it up and read to the end:

Thank you very much.